IN SEARCH OF
A HOMELAND
The Story of THE AENEID

PENELOPE LIVELY

IN SEARCH OF A HOMELAND

The Story of THE AENEID

Illustrated by IAN ANDREW

FRANCES LINCOLN

In memory of Frances Lincoln

British Library Cataloguing in Publication Data
available on request

ISBN 0-7112-1728-9

Set in

Printed in Hong Kong

1 3 5 7 9 8 6 4 2

CONTENTS

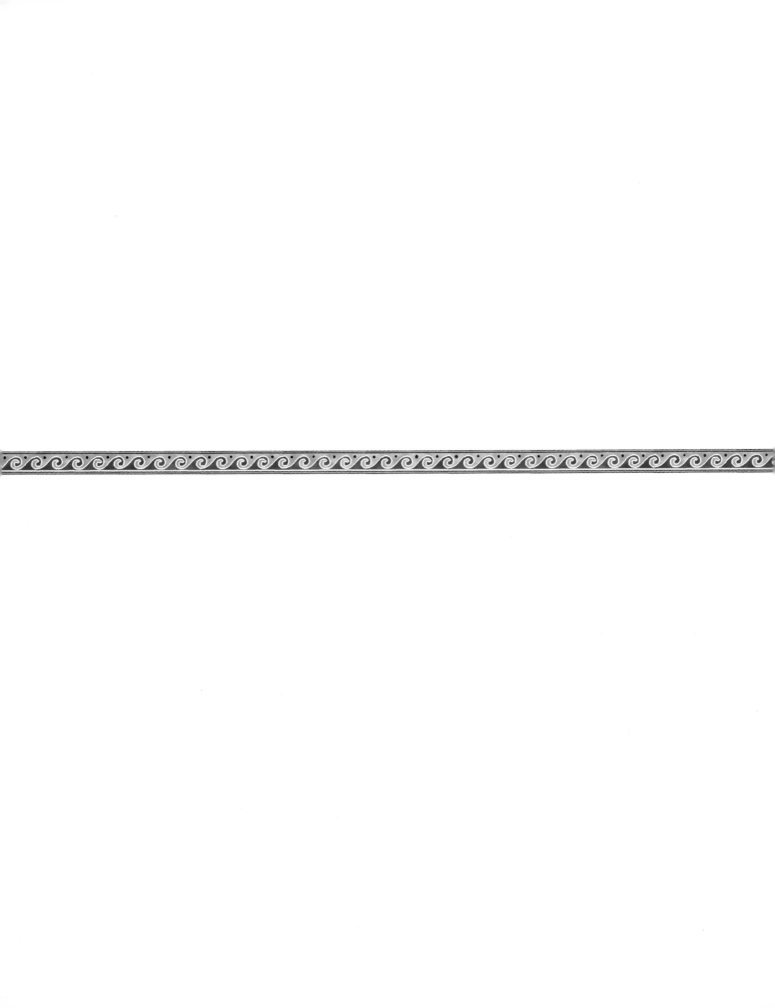

PROLOGUE

THIS IS A TALE OF WAR, and of the man who led the Trojan people across the seas and into their great destiny in the land of Italy. It is the story of noble Aeneas, son of Anchises and the goddess Venus, father of Iulus.

For ten long years the Greeks besieged the city of Troy, determined to seize back fair Helen, Menelaus' wife, who was lured from her Spartan home by the Trojan prince Paris. Time and again Greeks and Trojans had clashed on the plain before the city, with neither one the victor. Leaders had fallen on both sides: brave Hector, son of Troy's King Priam, and the golden Greek, Achilles.

At last the Greeks, weary of war and inspired by the goddess Minerva, devised a plan to put an end to the bloodshed. They built an immense wooden horse from pine logs and hid within its cavernous belly a force of their finest men, picked by lot. A tale was put about to reach the ears of the Trojans: this strange creature was an offering by the Greeks to Minerva to secure fair winds for their voyage home. Then the Greek ships set sail for the lonely island of Tenedos, not far off, where they settled down to wait…

THE FALL OF TROY

THE WATCHING TROJANS thought the Greeks had gone for ever. Joyfully they surged out of the city. The wooden horse stood massive and mysterious on the shore while the Trojans debated what should be done with this bewildering object: Drag it into the city, said some. But others were suspicious and cried that it should be burned or broken open.

And then Laocoön came running up, shouting in fury, "Fools! Would you trust a gift from a Greek? Are you crazy?" He flung his spear at the wooden flank of the horse and there came from within a hollow boom.

Alas, his shrewd warning fell on deaf ears. For his fellow Trojans were distracted by a further cunning ploy of the Greeks. Some shepherds had taken captive a stranger found wandering nearby, a pitiful-looking fellow who fell on his knees, begging for mercy: "Sinon is my name – a Greek, yes, but a victim of my own companions. I was their choice to be sacrificed to the gods, that they might smile upon my cruel comrades and allow them a safe passage home. But I escaped, and lay hidden in a marsh until I saw the ships depart. Have mercy, I beg of you – greater mercy than my own people have shown."

Thus did Sinon cringe and lie. The Trojans released his bonds at the order of King Priam, never suspecting that he was part of the whole clever scheme of the wooden horse, whereupon Sinon continued with his planned deception. "Spare my life, Trojans, and I will tell you how to save Troy. Remember how Ulysses and Diomede crept into your citadel and stole the Palladium, the image of Minerva, the Luck of Troy? The goddess was so angered at this outrage that she has set her face against the Greeks, whom she used to favour. They have sailed for Mycenae, to seek divine help. They will return. The great wooden effigy they left is an offering to Minerva to win back her favour. Destroy it, and you bring about the fall of Troy. Take it within the walls of the city, and the Greeks will themselves be shattered by war."

He finished speaking. And as he did so, a fearful sight brought cries of horror from the Trojan throng. All eyes turned towards the ocean as two great sea snakes rose from the waters, their coils and blood-red crests rearing above the waves. With blazing eyes and hissing tongues they made for Laocoön and his two young sons, twining themselves first around the children and strangling them in their terrible grasp, next seizing the frantic father as he ran to their rescue, and crushing the life from him while he howled in vain to the heavens. The monsters then slid up the shore and away to some secret lair behind the statue of Minerva in the citadel.

The Trojans watched aghast, and could only think that this must be a divine punishment on Laocoön for daring to throw his spear against the flank of the wooden horse. They resolved at once to do as Sinon advised, and tow the thing inside the walls of Troy before the goddess became further enraged.

Rollers were placed beneath the horse's feet, ropes tied around its neck, and the Trojans laboured to bring into the city the very instrument of their own destruction. Four times the great machine stuck fast in the gates, and the weapons clanged from within; four times the Trojans struggled to draw it onwards. At last the wooden horse with its hidden cargo came to rest within the heart of Troy. The Trojans then decorated all the shrines to the gods with garlands and went wearily to their beds.

Treacherous Sinon waited for the given sign – the flash of a fire signal from the sea telling him that the Greek fleet was on its way from the hiding-place at Tenedos. Then he stole through the darkness to the wooden horse, undid the pinewood bars in its side and released the silent warriors within. Down they dropped from the belly of the horse – first Thessandrus and Sthenelus and fierce Ulysses, then Acamas and Thoas, Neoptolemus, Machaon, Menelaus whose wife Helen was the cause of all this war and bloodshed, and finally the craftsman Epeus who had built the great horse. Stealthily they moved through the sleeping city. They fell upon the sentries, killed them before they could cry out, and opened the gates of Troy to their Greek comrades who now came pouring up from the ships.

The noble Trojan Aeneas lay asleep in the house of his father Anchises. He dreamed of the long years of war in which he had fought alongside his Trojan brothers and saw again brave Hector, filthy with dust and blood as he had been when dragged lifeless by the heels around the walls of Troy by victorious Achilles. But now, in Aeneas' dream, Hector stood weeping and urging him to flee: "All is over! The walls are captured, the city is in flames. The destiny of Troy lies in your hands, son of Venus! Take the sacred things of Troy, her household gods, and sail the seas until you find the shores on which you shall found the new city of our people."

Aeneas woke. With sinking heart he ran to the roof of the house, where he heard and saw the dreadful truth – the din of the stricken city, the shouts, the trumpets, the flames that roared like a forest fire or a river in spate. Reckless in his anger, he seized his arms and rushed forth to rally his comrades to the defence of their beloved city.

Aeneas quickly met with Panthus, Ripheus, Epytus and others, but as

they hurried through the narrow streets they soon realized how desperate was the Trojan plight. The Greeks were massed at the gates, the sentinels unable to resist them. Fires raged, Greek steel flashed already within the walls. The carnage had begun.

The Trojan band surprised and killed a Greek force and stripped them of their armour. Thus disguised, they were able for a while to wreak havoc among the invaders. They flung themselves to the defence of Priam's priestess daughter Cassandra, dragged brutally by the Greeks from the temple shrine. But in the confusion many were slain, some by their own fellows, who mistook them for Greeks. Aeneas and the other survivors now made for Priam's palace, where the fighting boiled with furious intensity. The Greeks stormed the building with ladders, their shields held above their backs; the Trojans tore up tiles and gold-plated roof beams to hurl down upon them. Aeneas shouted to his comrades to follow him up to the palace roof by way of a concealed entrance. There they put their shoulders to the look-out tower and sent it thundering down upon the attackers, but still the Greeks came swarming on.

The Greek Pyrrhus with his company smashed in the doors of the royal palace. The guards were cut down, the women fled screaming. In flooded the Greeks like a river that has burst its banks. And now Aeneas witnessed the tragic and terrible end of King Priam, who had snatched up arms to join the battle, grey-headed as he was. Pyrrhus slew young Polites before the very eyes of his weeping mother, Queen Hecuba, and her daughters. Priam cried out in rage and reproach and flung his spear. Pyrrhus swung round, fell upon the old man and dragged him by his grey locks through his own son's blood to the altar, where he thrust a sword into his side.

Aeneas moved in anguish through the palace, alone, his companions dead or in flight. His thoughts now were of his own father Anchises, his dear wife Creusa and their little son Iulus. What would be their fate? Blindly wandering thus, he came upon fair Helen herself, hiding in terror in a dark corner, she for whom Troy now blazed, she whose beauty had brought about this tragedy. And in his grief, it came to Aeneas that he would kill her rather than see her return unharmed to her home in Mycenae.

He drew his sword – but his divine mother Venus now intervened. She rose up radiant before him, urging him to stay his hand and instead to seek out his family. "Do not blame Helen! This is the work of the gods: Neptune, who shakes the wall of the city; Juno, who rallies her friends the Greeks; Minerva with the Gorgon glaring from her shield; and great Jupiter himself, who incites all against the Trojans. Escape! I shall protect you!"

The city was now blazing. Guided by his divine mother, Aeneas wove his way past gushing flames and through the sifting ashes to his father's house. Anchises, in his grief and despair, declared that he would not leave the city to seek safety in exile. At this, brave Aeneas prepared to go back into battle and certain death, since he would never abandon his father and family.

His wife Creusa wept, little Iulus clasped in her arms, and implored her husband to remain at their side. And as she sobbed and entreated, a strange thing happened. The cap worn by the little boy appeared to catch fire and a bright flame played harmlessly about his curls. Old Anchises, taking this for an omen, prayed to Jupiter for a sign. And, as though in reply, there came a crash of thunder, and a shooting star trailed sudden brilliant light through the darkness.

"The god has spoken!" cried Anchises. "Let us then depart."

Aeneas put a red-gold lion skin on his back and lifted his old father upon his shoulders. He took little Iulus by the hand, told Creusa to follow behind, and gave instructions to the rest of the household to meet with him at a certain hillock topped by an ancient cyprus tree, that stood beyond the city walls.

Aeneas made his way towards the city gates, his father upon his back and his child at his side. From the smoke and darkness all about there came the sound of rushing feet; a bronze shield flashed from a doorway. Aeneas quickened his pace, desperate now to save his loved ones.

And so it was that in the haste and confusion of the night Creusa was left behind to her fate. When they reached the meeting-place, she never came.

Wild with distress, Aeneas left his companions hidden in a valley and returned to the ravaged city. There he searched the silent streets, calling, "Creusa! Oh, my Creusa, where are you?" At last he saw her, and reached out his hand. But it was a wraith who stood there, a mournful ghost. Aeneas was struck dumb, his hair stood on end and his voice stuck in his throat.

"Dear husband," she said, "go – do not grieve for me. This is the will of the gods. Go now into the long years of your exile, for at the end will come good fortune and marriage to a royal bride." Three times Aeneas tried to take her in his arms; three times she melted at his touch.

Aeneas returned to his companions. Many more Trojan comrades had come streaming to join them, a forlorn army of the homeless, their city a smoking ruin.

The morning star was rising. Aeneas took his father up on his back once more and set out for the mountains.

THE WANDERINGS OF AENEAS

VENUS HAD SPOKEN. Aeneas knew that the task was his: he must lead his Trojan comrades in search of a new homeland, though none knew where they should go. They turned their backs upon the devastated city and set about building a fleet of ships. When summer came, the ships rode upon the water and old Anchises, their chieftain, urged that the sails should be raised and the Trojan survivors leave the shores of Asia in pursuit of their destiny.

They headed first for the nearby coast of Thrace, whose people had been friendly towards Troy, thinking perhaps to settle there. Aeneas made preparations for a sacrifice to the gods – a fine white bull to be slaughtered, an altar strewn with foliage. He was tugging at a tree to gather branches for the altar, when he was shocked to see dark blood gush forth from the broken root in his hand. In horror and dismay he pulled at other growths, whereupon there came sighs and groans from the earth itself, and a voice cried, "Do not rip my poor flesh, Aeneas! It is I, Polydorus, who lies here, slain by iron spears which have rooted in my body and turned to trees. Have pity on me, fellow Trojan!"

Aeneas was aghast, realising that his former comrade had been betrayed by this wicked land. Early in the siege of Troy, King Priam had sent Polydorus to the Thracian ruler with a great store of gold, asking him to keep safe both the treasure and the messenger. But when the Thracian learned that Troy was in defeat, he shifted his allegiance to the Greeks, murdered Polydorus and seized the gold.

The Trojans gave Polydorus a second and true burial, so that he should not wander for ever in the Underworld on the banks of the Styx. They piled the earth high upon his grave, made an altar dark with wreaths and cypress branches upon which the women, with hair unbound, offered foaming bowls of milk and sacrificial blood. And then they turned from this ill-fated place and sailed on once more.

The island of Delos, sacred to Apollo, used once to drift free upon the seas, until the god tethered it to the neighbouring isles of Myconos and Gyaros as a safe dwelling-place for men. The Trojans now made landfall here, carried by a fair wind.

Aeneas went at once to the ancient temple to pray to Apollo for guidance. No sooner had he spoken than the ground shook, the shrine appeared to open and a voice roared from within, "Hear me, O suffering Trojans! Do you seek your destined home? It is the land of your ancestors which shall receive you, and from there will the house of Aeneas rule the world. Search out your ancient mother!"

What was the meaning of this? To which city did the god direct them? The Trojans puzzled over these mystic words until old Anchises recalled that their ancestor Teucer first set sail for the Asian coast from the island of Crete. "It is there that we must go – to the kingdom of Knossos!"

Once more the Trojans weighed anchor. Their spirits soared, for rumour had it that the island was now deserted and would be ripe for them to occupy. They began to dream of the fair city that they would build and the homes that would be theirs, as the ships flew over the waves once more. Past Naxos they raced, where the Bacchantes dance on the hillsides, past Donusa and Olearos, past marble-white Paros and the scattered Cyclades. A following wind sped them on their way, and so they came to the ancient coastlands of Crete.

There Aeneas set about raising the walls of the longed-for city: Pergamea, he called it. Green spears of wheat rose from the fields, weddings took place, hearths glowed once more as the Trojans made their home.

And then disaster struck. Men, women and children were stricken with disease. The Dog Star blazed down, sending a drought that scorched the crops. Death and famine seared the new settlement. Anchises, in despair, could suggest only that they return to Delos and again seek help from Apollo.

One night, Aeneas had a vision as he slept — a dream of moonlit figures he knew to be the Trojan household gods, the precious trophies brought with them from the fallen city. The figures spoke: "We are sent by Apollo to give you comfort. You misunderstood the words of the oracle — Crete was never your destined home. There is another land, the land of the Trojan father Dardanus, a land that is called Italy. That is the true home of the Trojans and there you must lead us, great Aeneas, through all the hardships of this long exile."

Aeneas recounted the vision to his father in awe and hope. Anchises at once realised his mistake — he had confused the two lines of descent from which sprang the Trojan race. They must trust these words from Apollo, and be on their way once more.

And now a fearful storm brewed up. The sky became black, the wind whipped up the waves, lightning slashed the sky, rain poured down from the darkness. Palinurus, the helmsman, cried out that he could no longer tell night from day, and that he had quite lost his bearings. For three days the scattered ships drifted helpless on the rocking seas, before at last a coast was sighted, and the oarsmen churned the blue waters in their race for the shore.

The haven they had reached was a harbour on one of the islands of the Strophades. Here were green plains, with grazing herds of cattle and goats upon which the Trojans fell with glee and prepared a great feast, inviting the gods to share the plunder.

But they had not reckoned with the ancient inhabitants of the islands, the Harpies, who at once swooped from the hills with shrieks and flapping wings and a hideous stench. Grimmest of all monsters are the Harpies – birds with the pale ravenous faces of human women, talons instead of hands and foul matter oozing from their bellies. Time and again this terrible flock hurtled down upon the Trojans, snatching the food from their lips, until the Trojans seized their weapons and joined battle with the ghastly foe, sword and spear against claws and feathers.

At last the creatures withdrew, except for one: Celaeno, greatest of the Harpies, who perched on a high pinnacle of rock and screeched a prophecy: "Thieves! Invaders! Begone! Listen to me, Trojans! I know your fate – I have it from Apollo, who got it from Jupiter himself. Heading for Italy, are you? Well, remember this – there will be no home for you there, until you have suffered such hunger that you are forced to gnaw the very tables from which you eat!"

The Trojans stared up in dread at the horrid creature. Anchises prayed to Jupiter that this threat should not be fulfilled, and they prepared at once to flee from so ominous a place.

Onward sailed the Trojan band, past Zacynthus and Neritos, past Ithaca, the home of wily Ulysses. The rough winds of winter filled their sails, they coasted the shores of Epirus and set anchor at last in the harbour of Chaonia, below the city of Buthrotum.

Chance had brought them to the domain of a fellow countryman. Helenus, a son of King Priam, had built a city here. Heartened by this news, Aeneas went ashore to seek out his kinsman, and was amazed when he caught sight of Andromache herself, widow of Hector, grieving still for her slain husband and pouring a libation to his memory.

"Andromache, can this really be you?" he cried. And when Andromache had recovered from the shock of setting eyes once more on one she thought lost for ever, the Trojan heard the true tale of her swerving fortunes:

"Pyrrhus the Greek snatched me from the ruins of Troy and brought me here as his unwilling wife. In slavery I bore him a child, but when he tired of me he gave me over to his slave Helenus and took himself a Spartan wife. And thus came about his downfall, for her jealous lover slew him. On his death, a part of his kingdom came into the possession of Helenus, now a free man, my husband and founder of this Little Troy. So I am once more a wife of the house of Priam. But what of you and yours, noble Aeneas?"

Helenus himself came now to welcome the arrivals. Aeneas, deeply worried still at the evil prophecy of the Harpy, and knowing that Helenus was skilled in understanding signs from the gods – in reading the stars and the omens of birds and their flight – begged him to look into the future of the house of Anchises, and advise on the dangers ahead.

Helenus made a ritual slaughter of bullocks and then spoke with priestly and prophetic voice: "Arduous is the journey that lies ahead and grim are the dangers. The coast of Italy is far distant – first, you must skirt the whirlpool of Charybdis and the dreadful mouths of the monster Scylla. You must keep clear of Circe's isle and pass by the lakes of the underworld. Offer your prayers to Juno – if you fall foul of that dread lady you are lost.

When at last you beach your ships on the Italian shore, go first of all to Cumae and the sacred lake of Avernus. There you will find the priestess in her cave, the Sibyl, she who foretells the future by writing frenzied prophecies on leaves. But be warned! When the door to the cave is opened, the wind blows the leaves into fluttering confusion and the priestess never troubles to put the messages back into order, so that many who consult her go away disappointed, with no advice. Be patient – speak to her gracefully and beseech her to grant you a prophecy in her own voice."

The Trojans listened, intent, as Helenus finished, saying, "Above all, remember this. When, at a desperate time, you come upon a huge white sow stretched upon the ground with thirty white young at her teats, then you have reached the place that will be the site for your city."

Helenus now commanded that gifts should be brought to the Trojan ships – silver and cauldrons, a breastplate of chainmail woven with gold and a great helmet with crest and streaming plumes. Andromache gave to young Iulus robes embroidered with gold and a Trojan cloak, saying sadly that the sight of him reminded her of her own dead son Astyanax, slain by the Greeks when Troy fell. "Had he lived, he would be the same age as you."

Bidding a sorrowful farewell to their kinsmen, Aeneas and his comrades set out once more and, after some days' sailing, the watchful helmsman Palinurus steered them within sight of the heel of Italy. They cried out in joy to see the land that would be their home, though they knew that they were far away still from the shore destined for their landfall. Anchises offered up prayers to the gods, which were answered by a breeze that sprang up to send them speeding towards the temple of Athene, above a little harbour. And there Anchises took the sight of four shining white horses cropping the grass to be yet another sign: "Horses are the equipment of war, but they are also

harnessed for peaceful use. So if this land means war for us, then there is a hope of peace too."

On sailed the Trojans, sighting the gulf of Tarentum. Presently they could see Mount Etna rising above Sicily and hear the deadly sound of Charybdis, whose rocks suck down the waves thrice daily and then shoot them to the skies as though to lash the stars. Across the strait is Scylla, the monstrous creature, half woman and half sea-monster, whose many heads come snaking out to seize those who sail too close. The passage between these two is hazardous indeed; Palinurus stood steadfast at the helm and fought the treacherous currents to steer well clear of the cruel strait, and thus he brought the fleet safe to the shore of the Cyclopes. Here the harbour is calm, but Mount Etna roars nearby. Sometimes the volcano belches forth black clouds of smoke and hurls up balls of flame; at other times it spews forth molten rock. The Trojans spent the night in the woods, listening in terror to the fearful sound but not knowing whence it came. Mightily glad they were when dawn broke at last.

And now there came creeping from the forest a miserable creature, a man dressed in rags, with matted hair and beard, half-dead with hunger, who approached them begging for mercy. A Greek he was, Achaemenides, one of Ulysses' companions. His dreadful fate was to be accidentally abandoned in the cave of the Cyclops Polyphemus when the rest of his comrades made their escape tied beneath the bellies of sheep, after cunning Ulysses had duped the giant and put out his single eye with a red-hot stake as he lay in a drunken sleep. The wretched Greek had spent many months hiding from the Cyclops, who would rend a man limb from limb and gnaw his bones.

"Flee from here, and take me with you!" he implored the Trojans. "There are hundreds more like Polyphemus in these woods." And even as he spoke, they saw the giant himself come striding down the mountainside with his flock,

a hideous blind ogre steadying himself on a pine-trunk. Far out into the sea he waded, the waves never even reaching to his thighs, as he ground his teeth, moaned, and tried to wash away the blood that trickled still from the socket of his single eye.

The Trojans fled for their ships in terror, trying to be silent in their flight. But the giant heard the splash of oars and shouted for his brothers, so that the whole dreadful tribe came rushing to line the shore like a grove of towering trees. Desperate to escape, the Trojans would have headed off in any direction, but Achaemenides the Greek now guided them, remembering the course taken earlier by Ulysses. So once more they were able to keep well away from the hazards of Scylla and Charybdis, and arrived at last at the harbour of Drepanum.

And now there came a blow foretold neither by Helenus nor by the dread Harpy, Celaeno. Anchises died: the best of fathers, a noble chieftain. In grief they mourned the good old man – his son, his grandson and all the Trojan band – and lit his funeral pyre upon that alien shore.

A STORM AND A WELCOME

THE TROJANS PUT TO SEA, leaving Sicily behind them. They hoisted sail and raced over the waves, soon losing sight of land.

But Juno was watching them, nursing her resentment and brooding upon an old slight. The judgement of Paris rankled still, when Venus' beauty had been preferred to hers, and the seed was sown for her hatred of the Trojans. And now Troy had fallen, but some Trojans yet survived, bent for Italy where they would found a race to rule the world and challenge Juno's own chosen city of Carthage. For the goddess had the divine gift of knowing what the Fates intended and wondered how she could foil this destiny.

She fumed petulantly to herself. "All these years I have waged war against this race – am I to let myself be defeated now? I, Queen of the Gods, wife and sister of Jupiter?" Burning with anger, she turned to Aeolus, the god of the winds, who keeps their fury penned within black caverns beneath the mountains of his isle of Aeolia, where they howl behind bolted gates. "Help me, Aeolus! Unleash your winds! Let storms bring havoc to these men I hate, who would carry the household gods of Troy to a new home in Italy. I shall reward you – it so happens that I have fourteen sea-nymphs of unrivalled beauty – the loveliest of all shall be your wife."

Aeolus owed to Juno his favour in the eyes of Jupiter, so he was quick to comply. He struck the side of the mountain with his spear, and the winds came pouring forth. The sky turned black, thunder cracked the heavens, huge waves rolled across the ocean. Aeneas cried aloud in despair as he saw the ships flung far and wide. The south wind dashed three of them upon the rocks; the east wind drove three more on to a sandbank. Ilioneus' ship went down, and that of brave Achates. Men swam for their lives as wreckage swirled around them.

But now Neptune himself was aroused by the disturbance. He raised his head above the waves and perceived at once that this mischief was the doing of his sister Juno. In anger he summoned the winds: "Tell your master that it is not he who rules the oceans, but I.
How dare you! Begone!"

And even as he spoke, he calmed the heaving waves, threw aside the clouds and brought back the sun. He commanded the sea-god Triton and the nymph Cymothoe to push the ships from the rocks, while he himself lifted others from the sandbanks with his trident.

As the storm subsided, the Trojans made for the nearest shore, the coast of Libya. Seven ships only survived of the fleet and these now anchored in a landlocked haven. The weary men flung themselves in relief upon the sands, while Aeneas struck a spark from a flint and set about kindling a fire. Then he urged his companions to grind flour from corn they had salvaged and bake some bread.

Dark woods girdled the bay, interrupted here and there by rocky cliffs. Aeneas climbed to the top of one of these and gazed anxiously out to sea, searching for the ships lost from the Trojan fleet. None were to be seen. But in a nearby valley he spotted a herd of grazing stags. Here at least was meat for his companions. Fitting an arrow to his bow, he took aim; before long he had slain seven beasts, one for each ship's crew.

The Trojans prepared to feast, but before they did so, Aeneas set about rallying their spirits, concealing his own doubts and fears. "Friends, take heart! We have been through worse than this. Remember the Cyclops? Remember the Harpies? Destiny decrees that Troy shall rise again in Italy. We have only to endure the hardships thrown in our way and we shall win through."

The Trojans ate and rested. But elsewhere, the gods were once again taking a hand in their fate. Venus came complaining to her father Jupiter, bitter at the trials imposed upon the Trojans by Juno when Jupiter himself had long since promised that they would live to found the great race of Romans: "Misfortune hounds these men," she cried. "Is this how you reward their piety? Have you turned your face against them?"

Jupiter embraced his daughter and promised her that her people's destiny was assured: "Aeneas will fight a great war in Italy, and he will triumph. For thirty long years will his son Iulus reign, and he will found the city of Alba Longa. There for three hundred years his descendants will rule,

down to Romulus himself, from whom the Romans will take their name. The people of Rome will know no bounds in time or space, until even Juno will temper her anger and come to cherish them."

And with these prophecies the Father of the Gods sent down Mercury, his messenger, to inspire Dido, Queen of Carthage, ruler of those shores, with friendship towards the Trojans.

On the following day Aeneas set out with his trusted comrade Achates, to spy out the land and see what manner of place this was, and who were its inhabitants. Soon they came upon a young girl carrying a bow as though she were a huntress, and with her hair streaming loose in the wind and the folds of her tunic caught and tied above her bare knees. She called out to the Trojans to ask if they happened to have seen her hunting companions.

This apparition was Venus herself, disguised. Aeneas did not recognize his divine mother, though her beauty made him declare that surely she must be a nymph or goddess of some kind. Venus, however, insisted that she was only a simple Carthaginian maid. She told the men, "You have arrived in the land of Queen Dido, who came here from Tyre. A terrible history is hers. Her brother Pygmalion slew her beloved husband Sychaeus, coveting his riches. The crime was concealed from Dido until the victim came to her one night in a dream, a spectre with dagger wounds to his chest, who revealed his murderer and the hiding-place of the stolen gold. Dido fled for these shores with a band of faithful followers and the cargo of gold. So it came about that a woman led the Phoenicians here. Even now they are building the battlements and citadel of Carthage. But who are you, where have you come from, and where are you going?"

Aeneas began a sorrowful account of the Trojans' sufferings and of their long wanderings, bringing them now to this African wilderness with only seven ships left out of twenty. But before he could finish, Venus broke in: "See that flight of twelve swans, all in line? Listen to me, for I know how to read an omen. Just now an eagle swooped upon them, scattering them far and wide. But look! They are united again, gliding down to land together in long ranks upon the shore. So too are your ships coming safe to harbour. Go now – follow this road to the palace of the queen.”

Venus turned away. As she vanished, her beauty shone out and Aeneas knew her to be his mother. He cried out in reproach, “Always you visit me in some teasing disguise! Come to me as yourself – take me by the hand as your son!” But he spoke to empty air, tinted only with the rosy glow of the goddess.

Venus had not finished. As she rose again to the heavens, she used

her powers to wrap the two Trojans in a cloak of mist so that they came invisibly to the city of Carthage. They stood upon the hill above and watched in wonder. The Phoenicians swarmed below as busy as bees in summer, some laying out the foundations of buildings, others hauling stones for the citadel, yet more excavating the harbour and the theatre. Aeneas and Achates moved down into the heart of the city, still shrouded in their concealing mist, and reached the great temple to Juno that Dido was building. They gazed in wonder

at what they saw, and tears sprang to Aeneas' eyes. For there pictured upon the walls of the temple he saw the heroes and events of the Trojan war. There were Priam, Agamemnon and Menelaus. There was poor young Troilus in flight from Achilles, and there was Achilles again, selling back for gold the lifeless body of Hector. And there, indeed, was Aeneas himself in the press of battle, with the Greek leaders all around him.

But now Dido approached the temple, and at once Aeneas had eyes only for her beauty and her stately presence. She entered the precinct amid a throng of attendants – like Diana leading the dance along the ridges of Mount Cynthus, her quiver on her shoulder, a thousand mountain nymphs around her. Once seated on her throne, Dido began to receive delegations from her people and to direct them in their tasks, while Aeneas watched in wonder and admiration.

And now Aeneas saw to his amazement that amongst the crowd were his lost comrades – Antheus, Sergestus, brave Cloanthus and others of the Trojan company who had been swept away by the waves. Overjoyed, the two Trojans restrained their urge to rush forward in greeting and waited to hear more, hidden still in their shroud of mist.

They saw their comrades approach the Queen, Ilioneus acting as spokesman. With calm dignity he told her who they were and how they had been driven by storms on to this coast, frustrated yet again in the long struggle to reach their destination in Italy. But they had been given a rough reception by some of her people, who tried to drive them back on to the ships. "Aeneas was our king," he told Dido. "And if he is still living, you will not regret coming to our aid. Grant us sanctuary, we beg you, that we may repair our ships and continue on our way."

Dido spoke. "The name of Aeneas is well known to me, for who has not heard of great Troy, and the valour of her citizens? You are welcome here. This is a new kingdom and we are wary of strangers, but you are free to beach your ships. Depart when you wish, under my protection – or will you not stay here and share with us this city? Trojan and Tyrian shall share a destiny and be as one. If only great Aeneas were saved! We shall send envoys to search for him by sea and land."

The mist that enveloped Aeneas and Achates now melted away. Aeneas stepped forward, touched with his mother's divine glory, glowing with youth and vigour. He addressed the queen. "I am Aeneas the Trojan. I salute you, Dido – for you alone have taken pity on us in our ordeals, offering us sanctuary and partnership in your home and city."

Dido listened in awe, her head filled with all that she had heard of Aeneas' heroism and the perils he had endured. She replied, "I too have suffered. I too know misfortune. My heart goes out to you." And so saying, she led Aeneas to the royal palace, while giving orders for thank-offerings to the gods. There, preparations were made for a sumptuous banquet. A gift of wine was sent to the ships' companies down on the shore, along with bulls and fat lambs. Aeneas sent Achates down to the ships to fetch his son Iulus and to bring for the Queen presents rescued from Troy – a gold-embroidered cloak

and a dress with a border of yellow acanthus flowers, which had belonged to Helen herself.

Venus observed all this from afar. She brooded upon the threat of Juno's menacing intent, and a scheme came to her whereby Dido should be consumed with undying love for Aeneas.

She summoned her son Cupid, the winged god. "Listen carefully," she said to him. "Go to Carthage. There you must assume the form and features of the young prince Iulus, a boy like yourself. Then, when Dido takes him upon her knee, breathe into her the fire of love. I shall lull the real Iulus to sleep and keep him safe in my holy temple of Cythera until all is done."

Cupid sped earthwards. Within the palace the Trojan leaders were gathered, reclining upon purple draperies. The Carthaginians took their places on embroidered banquet seats, with Dido herself seated on a golden throne. Lamps hung from the gold-panelled ceiling, candles blazed in the darkness. A hundred maids and a hundred manservants replenished the tables with food and drink, brought water for the guests to wash their hands, carried bread to them in baskets. Dido looked with pleasure upon the gorgeous gifts brought by the Trojans. But she gazed with even greater rapture at young Iulus, and when he ceased to cling to his father and crossed the room to her throne, she hugged him close and could not bear to let him go, never dreaming that she caressed a god in disguise who would transform her heart.

Dido gave orders for a jewelled drinking bowl of heavy gold to be filled with the strongest wine. Calling upon Jupiter for his blessing, she first poured a libation upon the table, then passed the bowl around the company. Iopas took up his lyre and sang. When the applause had died away, the queen asked question after question about the Trojan wars, saying at last, "But come, noble Aeneas, tell us in your own words of the fatal trap set by the Greeks, and of the seven years of your wanderings."

And so, through that long night of feasting and talk, Aeneas told of the wooden horse of Troy, and of the death of Priam. He told of his flight with his dear father Anchises upon his back. He spoke of storms and famine. He told of the Harpies and of Scylla and Charybdis, and of the dread Cyclops. All at the banquet listened intently to the Trojan leader, but none more so than Dido. The doomed queen hung upon Aeneas' every word, for she was now far gone in love.

 # DIDO AND AENEAS

IDO WAS OBSESSED WITH thoughts of Aeneas: his voice was in her ears, his face before her eyes. She could not sleep. When dawn broke, she began to talk distractedly of him to her sister – of his looks, his valour, his divine descent. "Anna, sister Anna – what am I to do? For the first time since the death of my husband Sychaeus, my heart is stirred by a man. But I would rather that the earth open up to swallow me than that I should betray my vow to remain alone and true to Sychaeus." Her eyes filled with tears.

Anna spoke words of comfort. "Dear sister, why should you pine away your youth – without love, without children? Can Sychaeus desire this, from beyond the grave? You have indeed scorned suitors up till now – Tyrian chieftains and the African Iarbas, whose domains surround our city. But remember that we are threatened by war on every side – from neighbouring tribes, from your brother far away in Tyre. Marriage to the Trojan would secure our safety and ensure a great future for Carthage. Seek the blessing of the gods and keep this heaven-sent guest here beside you!"

Hearing this, Dido felt no more scruples. Fired by love and hope, she made the due sacrifices herself. She poured wine between the horns of a pure white cow, calling upon Ceres, upon Apollo and Bacchus and above all to Juno, goddess of marriage. She had sheep slaughtered and searched for signs among the steaming entrails. But what good were vows and shrines to a woman obsessed? The flame of love ate into the marrow of her bones; in her heart there was a secret wound.

Inflamed by passion, she roamed the city like a doe that carries the barb of some hunter's arrow. The walls rose day by day, and Dido would take Aeneas to view the work and then would seek to speak her thoughts, but always she choked back the words. Each night she would insist upon a banquet and further recital of the tale of Troy. And then, when Aeneas had gone, she would fling herself upon his empty couch – seeing and hearing him still. And in her terrible obsession she forgot about the building of the city: presently the battlements rose no higher, the soaring cranes stood idle.

Juno had been observing Dido's plight. She came to speak cunningly to Venus. "You've done well, you and that boy of yours – and what a fine fellow he is, to be sure – but what is the point now in continuing with our rivalry? Better surely to make peace and seal it by this marriage. You have had your way: Dido is poisoned with love. Let her become slave-wife to the Trojan, and you and I will share this nation."

Venus saw through Juno's words – that her true purpose was to thwart the destiny of the Trojans and keep them in Africa so that they might never reach Italy and found the Roman race. Smoothly she declared that she would not agree to this plan unless Jupiter himself were consulted.

Juno swept this aside. "Leave that to me. Listen: at dawn tomorrow Aeneas and Dido plan a forest hunt. I shall send a black cloud charged with rain and hail which will scatter their companions. The royal pair will take shelter in a cave and there I shall unite them in marriage, if you agree. That place shall be their wedding-bed." Venus agreed, and smiled deceitfully.

As Aurora's rays suffused the heavens, the hunting party stepped from the city gates. Dido's horse was decked out in purple and gold, she wore a purple cloak fastened with a brooch of gold, golden also were her quiver and the clasp that caught up her hair. And Aeneas, when he came to her side, carried himself with all the grace and glory of Apollo.

Young Iulus soon sped away in pursuit of a herd of stags, relishing his spirited horse and desperate to meet up with a boar, or with a tawny lion prowling down from the hills.

And then the sky roared and the rain fell. Each hunter, Trojan and Tyrian alike, sought his own shelter. Dido and Aeneas found themselves together in a cave and there, while the lightning flared, the heavens were witness to their union, which Dido would call a marriage, throwing secrecy aside and declaring her love.

Rumour now took a hand – that evil monster with a peering eye set beneath each feather, her ears forever pricked and her mouth with a myriad squawking tongues. By day she watches from the highest towers, by night she flies hissing between earth and sky, spreading lies and distortions as often

as she tells the truth. Now she made mischief throughout the cities of Libya, telling of Dido's shameless passion for the Trojan leader and how they whiled away the winter in each other's arms, neglecting all their royal duties.

King Iarbas heard this and was furious. He was the son of an African nymph ravished by Jupiter and had himself sought the hand of Dido. He had raised a hundred altars to his divine father, reeking with daily sacrifice. He now called upon him in a fury. "Almighty Jupiter! Do you see what is going on? I allowed this vagrant woman to build her little city on my territories. Now she has taken Aeneas as her lord, this second Paris with his youths who dance attendance on him. Will you stand by and allow this?"

Jupiter looked down. He saw the lovers lost in passion, forgetful of everything. He at once directed Mercury to fly to earth and intervene. "It was not for this," he said, "that Venus saved Aeneas from the Greeks. His destiny is to found the race that will rule the earth, sprung from Trojan blood. What does he think he is doing? He cannot linger here. He must set sail. Go and tell him my bidding."

Mercury laced his winged golden sandals to his feet and swept down from the heavens with the speed of wind, skimming the waves like a sea-bird until he reached the sandy shores of Africa. There he found Aeneas busy laying the foundations of the city, wearing a cloak of Tyrian purple woven with gold, made for him by Dido.

"For shame!" cried the messenger god. "Building a city to please your lady? Have you forgotten your destiny? Have you forgotten that other city which will be the ancestor of Rome? If you have lost the will to pursue your own salvation, then at least think of Iulus, your heir. Great Jupiter sends me to tell you this." So speaking, the god melted from human sight.

Shocked and shaken by this command — struck dumb, indeed — Aeneas knew that he must leave this land at once. But how could he break such news to Dido? In a torment of indecision he at last commanded his comrades to prepare the ships in secrecy. When the right moment came, he would speak with candour and with sorrow to the queen, and tell her that destiny and duty forced his departure.

But Dido in her heightened state was not to be deceived. News came to her of activity down among the Trojan ships, and she was flung into wild anxiety. She confronted Aeneas: "Are you planning to leave me without a word? What of our love and our promises? What of our marriage? What of the hospitality I have shown to you and yours? Would you abandon me to my enemies – rapacious Iarbas, or my scheming brother? I have not even a child – a little Aeneas – to keep your memory sweet."

Aeneas fought back his own distress and tried to calm her. "If only I were master of my own destiny… But you know that I am not. I never planned

44

to deceive you – do not think that. But I never made a marriage contract and I am bound to follow the commands of the gods. My grief is no less than yours, believe me, Dido. You have my love and gratitude. You will be in my thoughts for all time. The quest for Italy is not my choice."

Even as he spoke, Dido turned away, flinging an angry glance over her shoulder. Then her fury blazed. "Traitor! Hard as a rock you are, bred up by tigers rather than a goddess." She raved aloud, sometimes to herself, sometimes to Aeneas, silent now in his anguish. "Fool that I was to welcome a shipwrecked beggar! And does he shed a single tear now for one who loves him to distraction? Does he spare me a look or a sigh? Oh, I am driven to despair... And am I supposed to believe this tale of a message from the heavens? Have the gods nothing better to do? Oh, go, go, Aeneas... far be it from me to hold you back. Sail in search of this kingdom of yours. But I shall follow you. In death I will come to you – so shall you be punished." With this, she rushed away, to be caught up fainting by her maids and borne to her room.

In love and grief Aeneas saw her go, desperate to console her, but resolute in his determination that the gods must be obeyed and the ships prepared.

Down on the shore the Trojans were tarring keels, fetching fresh timber from the forests for oars and hauling the tall ships into the water. Dido watched in anguish from her citadel. Then, suppressing her pride and determined to make one last appeal, she summoned her sister Anna. "You always had his confidence, Anna. Go, I beg you, and speak to him as you know how. Ask humbly why he must make such haste. Ask him as one last favour to me to await a favourable wind. I do not ask for marriage, I do not ask that he abandon his destiny. I ask only for a respite in which to learn how to grieve. If he grants me this, I shall repay the debt with my death."

This sad message was carried to Aeneas. He too wept, but his will remained unbroken – he could not allow himself to be swayed by Dido's tears.

Now it seemed to Dido that she heard her dead husband Sychaeus calling to her from the darkness of night. In her dreams, Aeneas pursued her into madness, or else she travelled endlessly and alone, seeking for her Tyrian friends. So, possessed by grief, she prayed for death and calmly prepared the means.

She spoke again to her sister, asking her to have a pyre built under the sky in the inner courtyard of the palace, and to heap upon it Aeneas' arms that he left hanging on the wall of her room, the garments he wore. "For," she said, "I have taken counsel from a priestess skilled in questions of the heart. If all that reminds me of my betrayer is destroyed, then I shall be freed from my despair."

Anna, never suspecting her sister's intent, made haste to do as she asked. The great pyre was built from logs of pine and holm oak. Dido herself hung wreaths of flowers about the courtyard and covered the pyre with green branches. Offerings were made at the surrounding altars. Dido sent up a prayer to any power in the heavens with sympathy for those unhappily in love.

Night came, and with it blessed sleep. The seas were still beneath the encircling stars, birds and beasts were at rest. But Dido lay racked by her thoughts. What could she do? Beg one of her rejected Numidian suitors to marry her? Sail with Aeneas' ships and become a part of the Trojan destiny? But would they give her any welcome? And were she to do such a thing, should she go alone or force her Tyrian comrades to set forth once more upon the seas? No – there was no way out, save death.

Aeneas was sleeping in the stern of his ship, all the preparations for departure made. And now a vision of Mercury came to him again, uttering warnings of great urgency: "The queen is in a violent state and capable of any wild action. Do not linger! Hasten away before it is too late!"

Aeneas woke, terrified, and urged his comrades to their oars, himself striking the mooring ropes with his flashing sword. And so it was that with the first pale gleam of dawn, Dido looked down upon the empty shore and saw the Trojan fleet moving away to sea, their sails square to the following wind.

She tore her hair and beat her breast. She cried aloud for revenge – for weapons, for firebrands, for pursuit. "But what is the use?" she sighed. "I have brought this upon myself. I trusted him. I could have torn him limb from limb – faithless Aeneas! I could have had his comrades put to the sword, set his ships alight. I could have wiped out the house of Anchises,

then flung myself on the flames. Hear me now, O gods!" And Dido called on the heavens with a great curse upon her lost love. "May he suffer! May he be defeated in battle, may he be banished from his homelands, may he be torn from his son and see his people die! May he fall before his time and lie unburied on a lonely shore! And may there be war between my people and his for ever more – Phoenicians ever after seeking vengeance against the sons of Troy!"

Then Dido sent a message to her sister, speaking calmly so that none should suspect what she intended. "Tell my sister I go now to burn upon the pyre all that is left here of this man, and so to free myself from grief."

She burst into the inner courtyard. There she climbed the funeral pyre and took up Aeneas' sword. She spoke her last words. "So ends my span of life. I have founded a great city, avenged my husband and punished my evil brother. I could have been happy, had the Trojan ships never beached upon these shores. Now let me die, and may cruel Aeneas see from afar my funeral blaze and take with him the omens of my death."

And as she finished speaking, Dido plunged the sword into her breast.

The palace rang with lamentation. The city of Carthage wept as though ravaged by some terrible enemy. Her sister Anna climbed upon the pyre in anguish and held Dido in her arms as she lay dying.

And then Juno looked down in pity and sent Iris, goddess of the rainbow, to release Dido from her long agony. Iris flew down on saffron wings, trailing her colours across the sky. She hovered above Dido's head, saying, "This lock of hair I take as an offering to Pluto in the Underworld." And as she cut the lock, so Dido's life passed to the winds.

FUNERAL GAMES

FAR OUT AT SEA, Aeneas looked back towards Carthage and saw a great flame rise from the heart of the city. He was filled with unease and foreboding. But now a violent storm brought raging seas and a darkened sky. Palinurus the helmsman cried out that he would have to change course and go in the direction that the wind blew: "I cannot defy these driving waves and head for Italy. We must make for safe harbour in Sicily once more."

There the Trojans were welcomed by Acestes, son of a Trojan mother and the river god Crinisus. Down from the mountains he came, draped in a bearskin and slung about with javelins. He offered a gift of two oxen for each ship's crew, at which Aeneas called the whole company together: "It is a year

since my father Anchises died; near here
lie his bones and ashes. We shall honour his
memory now with funeral games – races between
ships and men, a shooting contest, and a boxing bout
for those who dare fight with rawhide gauntlets. But first,
let us all offer libations and a greeting at the tomb of my father."

At the tomb there came a strange omen. A snake slithered from
beneath the shrine, gliding forth in seven arching coils, his back
a gleaming blue and his scales gilded by the light. The creature slid
among the bowls and goblets, tasting the offerings but harming no one
before it disappeared. Was this the guardian of the place or, perhaps, Anchises'
spirit? None could tell.

Four heavy-oared ships did battle first. The captains stood on the high
sterns like charioteers, brilliant in purple and gold, urging on the garlanded
crews, whose naked bodies gleamed with oil. Neck and neck the ships beat
across the waves, until *Centaur* crashed against a rock and blue-green *Scylla*
sped into the lead, with her captain Cloanthus crying out to the gods for help:
"A white bull will I sacrifice upon your altars, O you who rule the sea!" The
god Portunus, hearing his cry, raised a great hand and pushed the ship
landwards swifter than the flight of an arrow.

Cloanthus was proclaimed the victor, and received as his prize a cloak
embroidered with gold and banded in purple, but when Sergestus brought

into the harbour his twisted and mangled *Centaur*, Aeneas bestowed on him as consolation the slave-girl Pholoe with her twin baby boys.

Now came the racing on land, in which the fleet-footed Trojan youths jostled – the friends Nisus and Euryalus aiding and abetting one another until everyone else cried out in anger. Aeneas laughed at their rivalry and declared that all should have prizes.

"And now," he cried, "Who is brave enough for the fist fight?"

Mighty Dares at once stepped forward and stood punching the air, while all hung back in silence, remembering his victories over men and giants. "The prize is mine!" jeered Dares, "for none dares challenge me!"

Acestes turned to Entellus, renowned once as the bravest of men. "Will you stand by and let him triumph like this?"

"If I were young still like that braggart," replied Entellus, "I would not need the offer of a prize to bring me forward." And so saying, he flung down the great gauntlets once used by the legendary hero Eryx, the famed fighter of ancient times.

The Trojans gazed in awe at the huge leathers, sewn from seven ox hides and stiffened with iron and lead. Dares, aghast, now shrank back from the fight.

"No wonder he flinches," said Entellus, "for these are the gauntlets with which Eryx stood up to Hercules himself. Let us level the odds. I will lay aside these famous trophies if he casts down his own Trojan gloves."

And so, freshly equipped with matching leathers, the two men fought it out – the one young and nimble, the other more powerful but watching keenly for the dancing blows that came now from one side, now another. Dares pressed hard and when Entellus was felled to the ground, Aeneas himself helped him to his feet. The older man fought back with renewed strength, his blood up. And when at last Entellus sent Dares spinning, Aeneas stepped forward again and parted the combatants. Entellus was awarded the victor's bull. He stood back and struck the creature dead with one blow of his mighty fist.

Now came the archery contest. A fluttering dove was tied by a cord to the top of a ship's mast to serve as target. Acestes was declared the winner, shooting an arrow so high into the air that it caught fire and flamed amid the clouds like a shooting star. And then, in glorious conclusion of the funeral games, the Trojan youths paraded on horseback before the whole company, weaving to and fro in movements of mock battle and retreat, like dolphins playing among the waves.

Meanwhile, Juno was once more in bitter mood. Her gaze fell upon the Trojan women waiting near the ships, and a scheme came into her head.

She sent Iris gliding down her many-coloured rainbow, directing her to take the form of Beroe, a respected Trojan wife. Thus disguised, Juno's messenger spread discontent among the Trojan women: "Seven years now! For seven long years we have roamed the oceans, homeless. Let us put an end to this misery. Let us set fire to the ships! Then there will be no choice but to settle here and rebuild Troy."

Her words inspired a madness among the women. They seized firebrands from the hearths and set the pinewood ships ablaze. Iris swept heavenwards again on her rainbow, her mission accomplished.

Aeneas and his companions saw the smoke and flames and came rushing to the scene. In a frenzy of despair, Aeneas sent up a desperate prayer to Jupiter, who took pity on them and sent down a quenching shower of rain. All but four of the ships were saved from utter destruction. The women, brought to their senses, hid in shame. But their action had much disturbed Aeneas and he was now in doubt as to what he should do. Wise old Nautes offered this advice: "Let those who are weary of our wanderings remain here and make themselves a home under the leadership of Acestes. You yourself, great Aeneas, must pursue your destiny to the shores of Italy with a chosen band of our people." This counsel was supported by the shade of his dead father, Anchises, who came to his son that night in a dream.

Aeneas put the plan to his comrades. Acestes welcomed the prospect of a city and at once selected the site of the forum. A temple to Venus was founded on the high peak of Mount Eryx and a priest appointed to care for the tomb of Anchises. The ships set sail with those of the Trojans determined to stay with their leader – Aeneas standing alone upon the prow, a goblet in his hands, from which he scattered wine and the entrails of three sacrificial calves.

Venus was watching. She enlisted the help of Neptune: "See how Juno continues to torment my people! Grant them a safe passage, I implore you!" Neptune heard her prayer and calmed the waves.

Aeneas' beloved comrade, Palinurus, stood at the helm of the leading ship. As night fell, the god of Sleep came gliding down from the stars. Disguised as Phorbas, he spoke honeyed words to Palinurus: "The seas are calm, the breeze is steady. Sleep... and let me take over the watch."

Palinurus replied that he would never trust his leader to the fickle winds, but even as he spoke, the god shook over him a branch dripping with the waters of Lethe and the river Styx, which bring forgetfulness and sleep. The helmsman's eyes began to close, and as sleep overcame him he plunged into the ocean, taking with him the broken stern and tiller. In vain did he cry to his comrades for help – none saw or heard him go. And when at last Aeneas realised that his ship was drifting, he took over the helm himself, crying out in grief, "Alas, Palinurus, you were too trustful of a calm sky and sea – now your body will lie naked on some alien shore!"

DESCENT INTO THE UNDERWORLD

THE TROJAN SHIPS BEACHED at long last upon the shores of Italy. They found there a coast of rocky crags and dense woodland parted by rushing rivers. The ships were moored with their curved stems fringing the shore, while Aeneas and a few companions made for the shrine of Apollo. It was here that Daedalus first returned to earth after he fled the kingdom of Minos: the Trojans gazed in wonder at the scenes depicted upon the golden doors of the temple he raised to the glory of the god. There was the Cretan city of Knossos, there the shameful union of Pasiphae and the bull with which she deceived her husband Minos. And there was their savage offspring, the Minotaur – half-man, half-beast.

Within the temple was a cavern with a hundred deep shafts from which the god speaks through the medium of his priestess, the Cumaean Sybil.

She came forth to greet the Trojans, bidding them to make sacrifices to Apollo, and when this had been done she led them into the temple. Here she paused upon the threshold of the cavern with a hundred deep shafts, from which the god speaks.

And now she became as one possessed – her colour heightened, her speech distorted, her hair disordered: "Ask for your destiny! The god is here!"

The Trojans stood awed and fearful as the frenzied priestess struggled with the power of the god, her body shaking and her mouth foaming. Aeneas cried out in supplication, "Phoebus Apollo, you have had pity for our sufferings. Grant my prayer. Allow us to settle here in Italy, according to our destiny."

The Sibyl's words boomed back and forth in the cave as she made her prophecy. "I see wars! I see the Tiber foaming with blood! A second Achilles awaits you, and another foreign bride. You must be bold and resolute."

And now Aeneas pleaded, "One thing I beg: let me descend to the Underworld, into the black realm of the god Dis. Let me go and look one last time upon the face of my father."

"Many enter that dread place," replied the prophetess. "but few return. If you dare make this journey, you must first find the golden bough that is sacred to Proserpina, goddess of the Underworld. She has decreed that all who visit her realm must bring as an offering a branch of that miraculous stem from which new leaves spring each time a growth is plucked. If it is your chosen fate to descend into the Underworld, then the branch will come away in your hand; if not, then neither strength nor cold steel will shift it."

Venus, ever-watchful of her son, now took a hand. She sent down two white doves, her sacred birds, which led Aeneas through groves and glades to a tree where gleamed the golden bough, twined around an ilex branch like a bunch of mistletoe. Aeneas reached up to the shining stem and it broke away at once.

With the bough secured, Aeneas hastened to Lake Avernus, which flanks the cave entrance to the Underworld. Here the Sibyl came to meet him, beside the black waters which throw up such noxious fumes that no bird can fly above them. The priestess sacrificed four black bullocks to Hecate, Queen of the Underworld, while Aeneas killed a black-fleeced lamb with his sword,

and a cow for Proserpina. He laid whole carcasses of bulls upon an altar for the Stygian king.

And as the sun rose, the earth roared beneath their feet and shapes like hounds howled from the shadows. The goddess was approaching.

The priestess told all to stand aside except for Aeneas. "Draw your sword, Trojan," she ordered, "and summon up all your courage!" So saying, she stepped into the dark mouth of the cavern, with Aeneas following fearlessly close behind.

In the very jaws of hell there swirled around them the spectres of Disease and Fear and Hunger. There was ashen Old Age, murderous War and mad Discord with bloodstained ribbons in her snaky locks. Monstrous creatures glared from the shadows – Centaurs, Gorgons, Harpies. There lurked the hideous Chimaera, a medley of lion, goat and snake. Aeneas drew his sword in fear, but his guide urged him onwards, and soon they reached the wide waters of the Styx. Here on the banks of the river was gathered a great throng of the dead, like flocking birds or drifts of autumn leaves, all with arms outstretched,

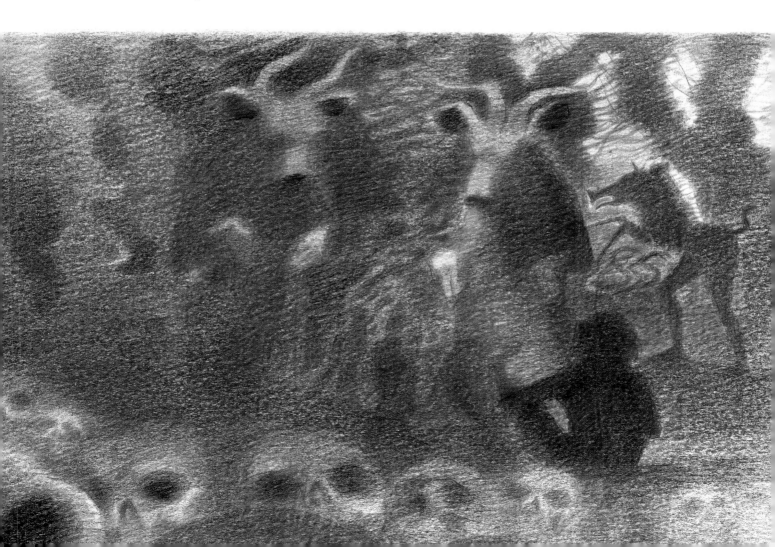

begging the grim ferryman, Charon, for passage to the further shore. But only those who have received burial may cross the Styx. The grey-bearded figure, clad in rags, was ruthless in his selection and pushed many away with his pole.

And look: the shade of Palinurus now approached. Aeneas greeted his dear comrade and heard how he had swum ashore, only to be slain by ruffians who left his body rolling for ever in the surf. "Have pity, Aeneas!" he cried. "Take me with you across the Styx!" The priestess would not allow this, but consoled Palinurus with the promise that a burial mound would be raised for his bones and the place where he died named in his honour.

But now Charon the ferryman challenged Aeneas: "None but the dead shall enter my boat! You are a living man!" The Priestess drew the golden bough from beneath her robes and, seeing the sacred offering to Proserpina, Charon agreed to give them passage. And so they crossed to the place where the three-headed dog Cerberus guards the cavernous entrance, snarling and snapping at all who come. The priestess threw him three honey cakes, which sent the monster into a deep sleep.

Soon the souls of those who grieve for all eternity surrounded them: the shades of children, snatched to untimely deaths; those unjustly condemned and those who killed themselves; and the mourning victims of unhappy love.

Wandering here in the great wood was Dido, her wound still fresh. Aeneas stopped, recognising her pale shadow as one sees the silver shape of the new moon rising through clouds. He cried out to her in love and grief: "Alas, unhappy Dido! So it is true – you are dead, and by your own hand? Was I the cause of this? Alas, alas! I swear to you by all the gods that it was against my will that I left you. Destiny drove me, as it drives me still. Stay, do not go. This is the last time that I can speak to you." He reached out towards her, weeping, but Dido refused to meet his gaze. She turned away and fled into the shadows where her murdered husband Sychaeus awaited her.

Aeneas and his companion came now to the most distant fields, set aside for brave warriors.

Here Aeneas saw many of his fallen comrades. Deiphobus was there, his body hacked and his face hideously mutilated in testimony of his terrible death. He told Aeneas of how Helen had signalled with a torch to the Greeks

on the night that Troy fell. The Greek dead were there too, and fled in terror at the sight of Aeneas, as though once more seeking to take to their ships.

The way ahead now divided. To the left lay Tartarus, the place of the damned. From within the city came the groans and cries of those who suffer eternal punishment – the evil-doers, the fraudulent, those who betray their kin. Rhadamanthus, king of Knossos, holds sway and the Furies torment the wretches held there.

To the right lay the road to Elysium. Aeneas fixed the golden bough to the gates of the city of Dis, in homage to Proserpina. Before them stretched the Elysian fields, a glowing paradise of woods and glades and meadows where live the brave, the good and those who have well served their fellow men.

Here at last Anchises approached with open arms: "You've come at last, my son!" Aeneas tried to embrace his father, but the phantom slipped from his grasp and led them to the valley where glides the river Lethe. Great companies of men and women stood upon its banks. "Here are those who will live again upon earth," said Anchises. "They drink of the waters of Lethe and thus forget their past lives. Their minds are freed from the prison of their bodies and will be reborn."

As Aeneas gazed in astonishment, Anchises climbed upon a mound. "Look carefully upon these souls, for I can show you the glory that lies ahead for the descendants of Troy."

He pointed:

"That warrior is Silvius, the son who will be born to you after your death.

Those are the men who will build fine cities for your race... and that is Romulus, who will found Rome in all her splendour, whose empire will rule the world.

There is Caesar himself, surrounded by all the line of Iulus... and there is Augustus Caesar, the man who will bring back a golden age to Italy."

So Anchises displayed the future to his son, the greatness awaiting the Trojan race, the heroes who would arise and triumph, the dominance of Rome. "Now remember this, Roman – your task will be to rule with authority. You must establish peace, show mercy to the defeated and subdue the proud."

Thus spoke Anchises.

But the time had come to say farewell. There are two gates of sleep – the Gate of Horn, which is the way out for true shadows, and the Gate of Ivory, through which pass false dreams. Anchises now sent his son on his way through the Gate of Ivory, back to the land of the living and to his companions in their ships by the shore.

THE FLAMES OF WAR

THE TROJANS SET SAIL once more. The fleet skirted the land of Circe, which echoes with the groans and howls of men transformed by the cruel goddess into wild beasts. Neptune guided the ships past that deadly coast and at last Aeneas sighted a great forest and the mouth of the river Tiber. Rejoicing, he ordered his comrades to steer for the shore.

The company was famished after the long voyage. Men were sent to scavenge for food and a meagre banquet of wild fruits and herbs was set out upon wheaten cakes. The hungry men devoured these makeshift platters also, so that young Iulus cried out in jest: "Look! We are even eating the tables from which we feast!"

His words brought Aeneas to his feet: "This was foretold by the Harpy herself!" he cried. And the Trojans remembered the angry screeching of the Harpy Celaeno from her rocky crag and realized with amazement and relief that her prophecy had come true. "This is indeed our destined landfall," said Aeneas. "Now truly we may make our home."

The city of King Latinus stood close by, and Aeneas despatched Ilioneus with a band of men to offer gifts and messages of peace, while he himself directed the building of a camp with surrounding earthworks.

Latinus was an old man, his only heir a daughter, as yet unwed. She was sought in marriage by princes from throughout all Latium, foremost among them the proud and handsome Turnus. But disturbing portents warned the king that his daughter must marry a stranger, one who would come from afar to join his blood with that of the Latins and raise their race to the stars. When Latinus heard from Ilioneus that Trojan Aeneas was come to his shores, he thought at once of these prophecies and his heart leapt. "Welcome, Trojans! Tell your leader I long to clasp him by the hand. I have a daughter. The Fates suggest that he and she are destined for one another."

Juno looked down from the heavens. She caught sight of Aeneas and his men busy at work upon the shore, their ships safe at anchor, and she was thrown into a rage: "Am I to be for ever thwarted by these defiant Trojans?"

She summoned Allecto, most fearsome of the Furies, she who fosters anger, war and hatred. Allecto came surging forth from her dark infernal home. She hurtled to the palace of King Latinus and there set about infecting his queen, Amata, with her own evil purpose. She plucked a snake from her black locks and sent it writhing and slithering about the queen, forming a necklace of twisted gold about her neck. The creature oozed fire and venom

into Amata's very being so that she cried out to her husband: "How could you do this! Our daughter is already pledged – to Turnus!" When Latinus paid no attention, Amata rushed from the palace and fled about the kingdom as one possessed, spreading wild rumours and whipping up resentment against the Trojans.

Now Allecto descended upon Turnus as he slept. She threw a burning torch into his heart, which sent rage and a lust for battle coursing through his blood. He woke sweating and shouting for his armour, and gave orders to his army to prepare to defend Italy by driving out these Trojan invaders.

Last of all the Fury sought young Iulus, who was hunting on the shore. The king's herdsman Tyrrhus had a tame stag; Allecto caused Iulus' hounds to pursue the animal, and thus Iulus, in all innocence, brought it down with a well-aimed arrow. The news of this offence spread far and wide, borne by Allecto herself. The country people rose in outrage. The Trojans streamed forth from their camp to the aid of Iulus, and so came the first clash of arms. Allecto flew back to her cavern, her wicked work complete.

The tribes of Italy now besieged the city of King Latinus, calling on him to declare war upon the Trojans. Latinus refused to do so. Hearing this, Juno herself flung open the city's Gates of War, with their hundred bolts of bronze. From every side the Italian warriors converged, eager for a fight, urged on by their leaders.

First to arrive was Mezentius, a ruthless warrior and one who despised the gods, with his son Lausus, who was second only to Turnus in youthful beauty. Aventinus was there, son of Hercules, and the Argive brothers Catillus and bold Coras. Messapus came, son of Neptune, and Clausus of ancient Sabine blood, leading his great army. Halaesus was next, with a thousand fierce tribes. Oebalus was there, and Ufens – famous for his feats of arms. Virbius, the son of Hippolytus, was sent by his mother Aricia.

Amidst them was Turnus, taller by a head than any other. A Chimaera breathed fire from his triple-plumed helmet; on his shield there shone in gold a figure of Io, the princess of Argos changed into a heifer by Juno. And all around him there surged a great horde of foot-soldiers and columns of armed men, who came pouring from fields, from plains and from the banks of the river Tiber.

Last of all came Camilla, warrior maiden of the Volsci, royally robed in purple, her hair caught in a gold clasp, a lance of myrtle wood in her hand.

 # THE FUTURE FORETOLD

THUS WERE THE FLAMES OF WAR kindled throughout Latium, with young warriors howling for blood. Aeneas was sick at heart. He went to sleep alone that night on the banks of the Tiber, beneath the calm vault of the stars, and there Father Tiber himself came to him in a dream. The god rose from the river, wrapped in a blue-green cloak and with dark reeds in his hair. He spoke words of solace: "Long have we waited for you, Trojan. Here is your rightful home. Fear not the threat of war, for the fury of the gods is spent." And he told Aeneas that he must take a picked force of men and row upstream to where Evander, king of the Arcadians, had his city close by the river. "For," he said, "his people wage perpetual war with the Latin race and will be your allies."

The river-god plunged to the depths of a deep pool.

Aeneas awoke to the first rays of the rising sun. He cupped water from the river in his hands and offered a fervent prayer of thanks. Then he manned two biremes from the fleet with oarsmen and an armoured company of his comrades.

No sooner had they set off, than Aeneas spotted through the trees the sight promised long since by Helenus. There, lying beneath ilex trees on a shore of the river, was a great white sow with a litter of thirty piglets! This was the sign that in thirty years time young Iulus would found the city of Alba, the ancestor of Rome itself. Aeneas made a sacrifice of the animals to Juno, that she might cease her persecution of the Trojans.

For a day and a night the ships slid swiftly upstream, speeded by Father Tiber. The warriors' shields glinted in the sun and the painted prows shone out as the Trojans navigated the winding waters, until at last they saw in the distance the scattered roofs of houses and the walls of a citadel.

The Arcadians were not a wealthy people. They lived in simple fashion under their king Evander, who that day was making sacrifices to mighty Hercules in a glade beyond the city walls, attended by his senators and his son Pallas.

Seeing the tall ships glide down the river, they were seized with fear. Brave Pallas snatched up a weapon and rushed to confront the strangers: "What race are you? Where do you come from? Do you bring peace or war?"

Aeneas replied from the high poop of his ship, holding out the olive branch of peace, "We are Trojans – exiles hounded by the Latins. We come in search of King Evander, to ask for his help in battle."

Evander received the Trojans with joy, recalling Anchises and King Priam himself, who visited the land of Arcadia long ago. He ordered a feast to be set out upon the grass in a grove for both his visitors and his own people. He himself sat with Aeneas upon a couch of maple wood cushioned with a lion skin, and there he told the Trojans the story that lay behind this annual ritual of sacrifice to Hercules.

"Once, my people were plagued by a foul monster, Cacus. See that black cavern up there among the rocks? That was his home. The pale and rotting heads of men were nailed to the entrance and the floor stank of his victims' blood. The god Vulcan was Cacus' father and he spat black fire from his mouth when he surged further from his lair. For many years we endured his persecution, until great Hercules chanced to pass this way, driving a herd of cattle through our land.

"The monster Cacus crept forth and stole from their pasture four bulls and four heifers, dragging them to his cavern by their tails so that their hoof prints should not betray the theft. But a single heifer lowed from the depths of the mountainside in response to the calls of the herd below. Hercules blazed with anger and snatched up his great knotted club. Cacus was afraid for the first time in his life. He fled into the cave and blocked the door with a huge boulder suspended on chains, created by his father's art. Three times Hercules tried to force the rock aside;

three times he circled the Aventine hill in fury and frustration; three times he dropped down exhausted in the valley.

"But now Hercules climbed to a ridge above the monster's den. He set all his immense strength against a tall needle of flint that rose from the rocks, loosened it, wrenched it free from the ground and sent it hurtling into the valley. The cave of Cacus was unroofed; light gushed from above into the shadowy cavern below, and there was Cacus howling and vomiting black smoke from his hideous jaws. Hercules threw rocks and trees down upon him and then, losing patience, leapt upon the brute and clenched him by the throat till his eyeballs sprang from their sockets and his blood ceased to flow in his veins.

"And so we were freed from this monstrous tyranny, and we celebrate the god each year on this day."

When the sacred rites were complete, the old king led his visitors back to the city, saying as they went, "Long ago, these woods were the haunt of fauns, nymphs and a race of men born from the strong wood of oak trees. They were hunters and gatherers, with no knowledge of farming or a settled life. Then the god Saturn arrived, in flight from the enmity of Jupiter. He brought the mountain people together, gave them laws and reigned over them for many peaceful years. But this golden time was overtaken by another age, when men were filled with greed for riches and with the lust for war. Bands of Ausonians and Sicanians arrived; the land lost its ancient name of Latium, given by Saturn. Then Fortune and Fate, who direct all our lives, brought me here."

And now, as King Evander led them through woodland and rocky outcrops, it was as though this Arcadian spot whispered the secrets of its great future. For it was here that Rome herself would arise. There was the Carmental Gate, named in honour of Evander's mother, the nymph Carmentis, first to foretell the glory of the sons of Aeneas. There was the grove that Romulus would set up as a sanctuary, the Asylum. And there beneath a cool rock was the Lupercal. Evander led his guests to a place of grass and bushes where one day the house of Tarpeia and the Capitol would shine out in gold. "There is some divine presence here," he told them. "The country people walk in fear and say that they have seen Jupiter himself shaking his dark shield to drive the storm clouds. And here too are the ruined citadels of two towns – one founded by Saturn, the other by Janus, the two-faced god."

They arrived soon at old Evander's modest home. And here again they walked amidst the ghostly landscape of another world to come, as cattle lowed where the Roman Forum would arise. "My home is humble," said the king. "But Hercules himself stooped to enter here." Within was a leafy bed covered with the skin of a Libyan bear, and here Aeneas laid himself down to sleep, as the dark wings of night enfolded the earth.

The whole company rose early, when the dawn chorus of birds was lifting from the trees. And now Evander solemnly pledged his support to the Trojans: "You are favoured by the Fates, great Aeneas. You are chosen by the gods.

This war is decreed so that the name of Troy may live for ever more, Go now… and I send with you my son Pallas and four hundred picked horsemen. The Etruscans too will rally to your cause, for they have suffered the harsh oppression of cruel Mezentius, who is Turnus' ally."

Venus now sent a sign. From a clear sky there broke great peals of thunder as clouds gathered and lightning flashed. From amidst the darkness the bronze glow of armour was seen and the clash of metal split the heavens. Aeneas understood at once, and cried out, "The goddess my mother sends this portent of war to come. The Ausonians have broken the peace and must beware. Turnus will get what he deserves."

Aeneas despatched some of his company to sail downstream to the Trojan camp and give news of this alliance. He himself would go with a chosen band to the king of Etruria. Old Evander embraced the young prince Pallas. "May the gods keep you safe, my dear son. May I live to see you again." So saying, the frail old man collapsed and was borne away by his attendants.

The Trojan force rode forth from the gates of the city, with Pallas proud in their midst. They took the shortest route and the beat of their horses' hoofs drummed at a gallop across the dusty plain. At a glade by the river they stopped for rest and refreshment.

And now Venus herself came to her son as he stood apart from his comrades. The goddess had been busy. During the night she had visited her husband Vulcan, the smith of the gods. Deploying all her charms, she put her white arms around him and spoke soft words of entreaty, begging him to use his art to make armour for Aeneas. Vulcan, always in thrall to her beauty, embraced her until the dawn, when he went in search of his Cyclopes, to set them to work.

Beneath an island of smoking rocks off the coast of Sicily are the great caves in which the Cyclopes have their forges. Here they work in a vast cavern which echoes with the sound of blows upon anvils. The furnaces blaze and the bars of red-hot metal hiss as they are plunged into water.

Here came Vulcan and ordered the Cyclopes to abandon their work – a chariot for Mars, polished armour for Pallas Athene. "I have a task for you," he said. "Arms fit for a hero. To work!"

When all was done, Venus came to her son. "Here are the gifts I promised you."

There was a great crested helmet and a death-dealing sword, a breastplate of dark bronze and polished greaves. But most wonderful of all was the shield, for upon its gleaming surface the God of Fire had depicted the great future of Rome. There was told the story of Roman triumphs, and there in sequence were the generations that would spring from young Iulus.

The mother wolf that suckled Romulus and Remus lay stretched out with the twin boys at her udders. The Sabine kings made sacrifices before the altar of Jupiter to ratify the treaty that ended their war with Rome. Deceitful Mettus was ripped in two by four-horse chariots. Here was Porsenna ordering the Romans to take back Tarquin after his expulsion, and here was his siege of the city.

At the top of the shield Manlius, keeper of the citadel, kept watch from the heights of the Capitol. And there, picked out in silver, was the goose that warned of the encircling Gauls, and there were the Gauls, creeping up in darkness through thickets of thorn. The dancing priests were shown, the Salii, and the naked Luperci with their shields that fell from heaven. Matrons in cushioned carriages led sacred processions through the city. Elsewhere was the gateway to hell; Catiline hung from a crag, trembling before the Furies. And in a place set apart for the righteous, Cato drew up laws that were just and fair.

Between these scenes there ran a swelling golden sea, showing blue depths beneath the white crests of waves; silver dolphins played upon the surface. In the very midst were the bronze-armoured fleets at the battle of Actium, with Augustus Caesar radiant upon the poop of his ship – and finally he was portrayed entering the walls of Rome in triumphant procession, three times a victor.

Aeneas stood marvelling. The meaning of this divine creation was mysterious to him, but he stooped and took up the shield, lifting upon his shoulder the destiny of his people.

NISUS AND EURYALUS

ALL THIS WHILE, THE REST of the Trojan company waited in their camp by the shore, young Iulus amongst them, anxious for his father's return.

Juno saw that it was time once more to take a hand. She sent Iris swooping down her rainbow to seek out bold Turnus, appointed commander of the Latin forces. "Attack the Trojans now, Turnus! Now is the moment to strike, while Aeneas and his companions are far away!"

Turnus seized on this advice. The Trojans, watching from their ramparts, saw a gathering cloud of darkness as the Latin armies surged across the plain. Soon men, horses, chariots were swirling all around and they could see Turnus himself taunting them to come out and fight, a towering figure in golden helmet plumed with red, riding a piebald horse. But the Trojans had been ordered by Aeneas to avoid pitched battle. They stayed behind their gates, fearful but resolute.

Turnus stormed up and down before the Trojan ramparts in rage and frustration. "Fire their ships!" he ordered. "That will smoke them out!"

The Latins rushed to the beach with blazing firebrands. But as they prepared to fling these into the anchored vessels there came a miraculous intervention. Jupiter himself spoke from the heavens: "Fear not, Trojans. Your ships shall be saved. Go now – you are freed!" And at his command the ships snapped their ropes, plunged like dolphins to the depths and rose from the sparkling waters changed into sea-nymphs.

The Latins were astonished. Even bold Messapus was dismayed. But Turnus was undaunted. Encouraging and exhorting his forces, he next ordered a siege of the Trojan camp. And so, as night fell, the whole rampart was encircled with glowing watch-fires as the Latin armies settled for the night.

Darkness fell. The Trojans checked their defences and set armed guards on the ramparts, each man taking turns at the points of greatest danger. Their commanders gathered in the heart of the camp to confer. What was to be done? How could they get word of their plight to Aeneas?

As they talked, leaning upon their spears beneath the glittering stars, those two young comrades, Nisus and Euryalus, came running up in great excitement, offering to put forward a plan. Encouraged by Iulus himself, Nisus burst out with their scheme: "Our enemies out there lie in a drunken sleep, for the most part. Their watch-fires are all around, but we have found an unguarded gap. Let us go under cover of the night and search for Aeneas and his company."

The Trojan leaders saw at once that this was a brave and dangerous enterprise – some might say rash. There was doubt and hesitation, but then wise old Aletes spoke: "Let them go! Such valour should be encouraged."

Young Prince Iulus broke in: "My hopes for our future will be in your hands. Call back my father. And when at last victory is ours, you shall be rewarded. The scarlet plumed helmet worn today by Turnus shall be yours, with his shield and his horse. More than that, you shall be my chosen comrades for ever more."

The young friends were escorted to the gates of the camp by the Trojan leaders. There, they slipped out into the night, crossed the ditch and crept with drawn swords among the Latin armies – among the chariots, the tethered horses, the wine cups flung upon the grass, the men sprawled in drunken sleep.

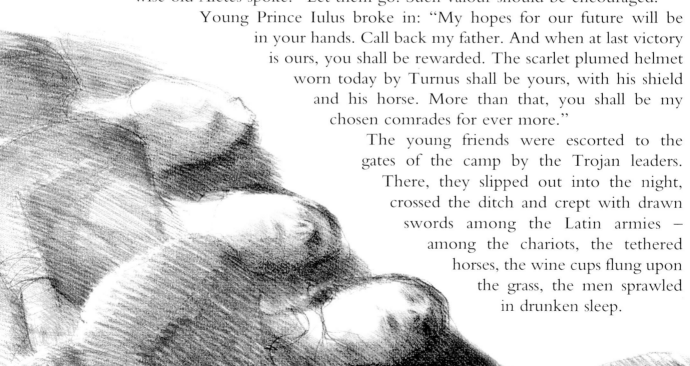

Nisus and Euryalus moved like shadows,
unseen and unheard. The sight of their unwary
foes filled them with a wild and fatal lust for blood.

Nisus was the first to strike, falling upon proud King Rhamnes, propped snoring on a pile of rugs. His attendants were the next to roll headless upon the grass, then Lamyrus, Lamus, young Serranus... Blood spurted upon the ground amid the dying embers of the watch-fires.

Euryalus too was busy. He slaughtered Fadus, Herbesis, Abaris... Rhoetus woke, saw in a dazed panic what was happening, went to hide – but received a sword up to the hilt in his chest before he could escape. Soon Euryalus was approaching the campfire of Messapus and his entourage, but Nisus came running up to call a halt. "Enough! Daylight is coming – we must be on our way!"

But now disaster struck. Volcens had been sent out with a detachment of cavalry and was returning to report to Turnus. The glitter of moonlight on Euryalus' helmet betrayed the Trojan pair as they fled. "Halt, who goes there?" shouted Volcens.

The two friends plunged into the woodland. The enemy horsemen instantly spread out, cutting off all lines of retreat. Nisus became separated from Euryalus as he rushed through the trees. Then shouts of triumph told him that his friend was captured. In anguish, ignoring his own fate, he turned and headed for the sounds of action. He flung his spear and by a lucky chance brought down one of Volcens' men.

Carnage ensued. As Volcens approached Euryalus with his sword drawn, Nisus burst out from the trees, crying, "Here I am! I did it. It's all my fault!" Volcens fell upon Euryalus in a fury and sent his sword through his ribs. Then he turned to meet Nisus. The two clashed, eyeball to eyeball, weapon to weapon, and fell dying at each other's hand.

The saffron light of dawn broke upon the night's bloody work. The Trojans behind their ramparts were faced with the sight of the heads of Nisus and Euryalus paraded before them on the points of Latin spears. Great was their sorrow and loud the weeping that rose from the Trojan camp. But there was no time for mourning, for now came the first attacks from the massed Latin armies.

A phalanx of Volscians stormed one part of the rampart in tortoise formation, their shields locked above their backs in defence against the rocks that the Trojans rained down upon them from above. Elsewhere, Mezentius was brandishing fire and smoke from a great torch of pinewood. Messapus called for scaling ladders.

Turnus, leading the assault, flung a flaming brand which set fire to a high wooden tower. As it tumbled, the ramparts were breached, and now there was hand-to-hand fighting between Latin and Trojan.

As the battle raged, young Iulus, inflamed by the taunts of Remulus, a kinsman of Turnus, could restrain himself no longer. He fitted an arrow to his bow and put an end to this cocksure mockery. He would then have flung himself into the fray, had Apollo not looked down and seen Remulus fall dying and Aeneas' son about to put his life in danger. The god quickly took on the form of Butes, a respected Trojan elder, and spoke to Iulus: "Enough, my boy. Your time has not yet come." His comrades, recognizing the god, held back the son of Aeneas from further risk.

Proud Turnus was everywhere, raging from one part of the battle to another. He surged through the ramparts, a fearsome figure dealing out death and destruction, the red crest of his helmet lifting above the throng of warriors. And there within the Trojan camp he was challenged by mighty Pandarus, giant among men. He raised his arm, held steady, flung his spear at Turnus – in vain, for Juno reached down from the heavens and brushed it aside. So Pandarus died, felled with one blow of Turnus' sword.

Now Turnus slew Trojans right and left, within the very walls of their camp. Those trying to oppose him fell back before his whirling sword. Mnestheus and Serestus, so valiantly leading the Trojan resistance in Aeneas' absence, hurried to the scene in dismay to fire their men. "This is our final stand – there is no retreat! Have you no spirit, no shame!" they cried.

The Trojans rallied. Their whole force was now flung against one man, against the towering figure of Turnus. They massed around him like a crowd of huntsmen advancing on a cornered lion, with levelled spears. Still Turnus fought on, giving ground against the hail of weapons, sweat pouring from him, panting for breath.

At last he could hold out no longer. He turned and dived head first into the river which swept him away, jubilant, to join his comrades.

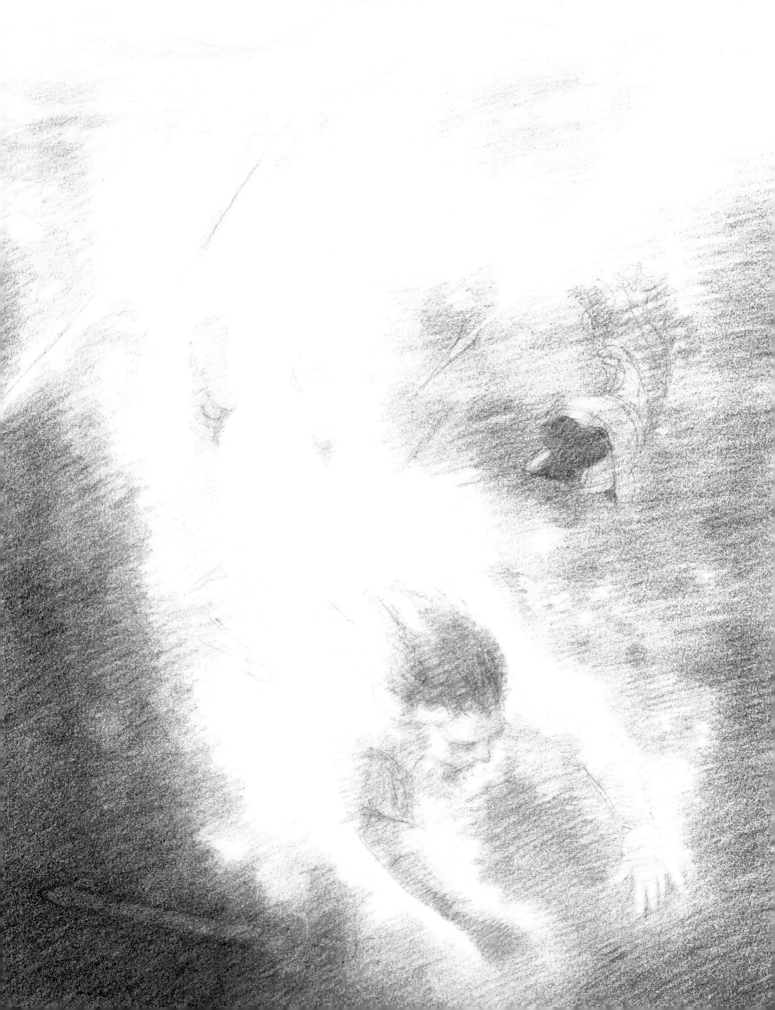

THE RETURN OF AENEAS

THE TROJANS WERE TRAPPED within the ramparts of their camp, unable to escape and far outnumbered by the enemy who swarmed around them. And Aeneas, still far away, knew nothing of the plight of his comrades.

In his palace amid the stars of heaven, Jupiter summoned a council of the gods and berated them for stirring up discord among men, for setting Latin against Trojan. "The time will come soon enough for war, when barbarous Carthage rises against Rome. For now, let there be peace!"

Golden Venus at once spoke up. "But the Trojans are in desperate straits! Have they not suffered enough? Their destiny is in Italy — surely that was your own command! It is cruel Juno who would drive them from the face of the earth. Have pity on them, I beg you!"

90

Juno burst out in a fury. "Destiny indeed! Aeneas was launched on this course by the ravings of Cassandra, in the ruins of Troy! And how is all this my doing, may I ask? Why is it right for the Trojans to sweep into the lands of others, to cheat Turnus of his bride? And who spirited Aeneas away from the victorious Greeks? Who lends him a hand at every turn? It is too late now for your complaints and lies!"

The gods began murmuring among themselves, some taking the side of Venus and others preferring Juno, until Jupiter silenced them. "Enough! So be it! I shall favour neither side. The Fates will decide the outcome!"

While the thin line of defenders on the ramparts struggled to hold back the besieging armies, Aeneas was speeding across the seas. The Etruscan king Tarchon had instantly given Aeneas his support and sent chosen leaders

with thirty ships to the aid of Troy. This fleet now ploughed the waves, with Aeneas' own vessel in the lead, a pair of carved lions cleaving the waters beneath the figurehead. There sat great Aeneas himself, with young Pallas at his side.

Massicus, on the bronze-plated *Tiger*, brought a thousand warriors. Grim Abas came, with the gilded figurehead of Apollo shining from his ship. Asilas too led a thousand men with bristling spears. Astyr was next, with a force of three hundred. Then Cunarus. Cupavo's ship bore a centaur as its figurehead, making as though to hurl a massive rock into the waves. Ocnus sailed too. And lastly Aulestes, in the great ship *Triton*, with a figurehead half-man, half-beast, its belly ending in a monster of the deep.

As Aeneas sat, sleepless, with his hand on the tiller, searching for the shore where he would be reunited with his comrades, he saw a miraculous sight. A line of sea-nymphs came dancing towards his ship. He watched in bewilderment as the leading nymph, Cymodocea, lifted herself above the water to place her hand on the stern of the ship: "Do you not know us, Aeneas, son of the gods? We are your lost fleet, the ships that dived like dolphins beneath the waves, when Turnus threatened us with fire, to rise again transformed. But you must hasten. Your comrades and your son Iulus are besieged and in a desperate plight. The cavalry sent by Evander and by the Etruscan king has arrived upon the plain, but Turnus and his armies have prevented them from relieving the Trojan camp. Take up your invincible shield made by Vulcan himself and hurry to your friends!" And so saying, she gave the ship's stern a push with her right hand, so that at once it flew over the waves like a javelin or a wind-borne arrow, followed by the rest of the speeding fleet.

Once within sight of the shore, Aeneas raised his shield towards the sun and flashed a signal to his comrades in the camp. A great cry of greeting and of hope went up from the ramparts. The Latins saw with amazement that the sea was alive with ships, and in their midst the gilded figure of great Aeneas himself, his helmet and his shield flaming above the blue water.

Turnus was undaunted. He at once directed his men to line up along the shore and repel the Trojan landing.

Trumpets sounded. The battle began. Aeneas was the first to move boldly against the Latins. Many fell to his sword – tall Theron, rash enough to challenge him, Lichas and Cisseus and Pharus. Spears hissed around the Trojan hero, some bouncing harmlessly from his helmet or shield, some deflected by his watchful mother Venus. The fighting whirled hither and thither – along the shore, on to the plain – with Trojans and Latins buffeting one another like opposing winds. Hand to hand they fought, eyeball to eyeball.

Pallas, son of King Evander, saw his Arcadian force driven into retreat and hurried to rally them. As he turned the tide of battle with his shouts and brought his men streaming back to the fight, Mezentius' son Lausus saw what was happening. He came forward himself to confront Pallas, his equal in youth and nobility.

Venus hovered in protection of her son. But Turnus was not without divine support, for his sister Juturna, the goddess of springs and streams, kept watch for her brother. When he learned from her of the confrontation between Lausus and Pallas, he came racing in his chariot from another part of the battlefield: "Pallas is mine! Leave him to me!"

Turnus leapt from his chariot to engage in close combat. Pallas hurled a spear which merely grazed the Latin. And now the spear flung by Turnus found its mark, driving through the centre of Pallas' shield to pierce his heart. So fell the son of Evander, and Turnus, placing his foot on the dying youth, tore the massive sword-belt from his body as victor's spoil.

Aeneas burned with grief when he heard of this death. He raged through the battlefield like an angry lion, hunting for Turnus. Those who dared confront him were cut down. Many Latin leaders fell to his sword, others he took prisoner for sacrifice on the flames of Pallas' funeral pyre. The brothers Lucagus and Liger, driving a chariot drawn by two white horses,

were fools enough to taunt him – "Today you will die, Trojan!" Aeneas caught Lucagus in the thigh with his spear, snatched the horses' bridles and struck Liger with his sword, even as he begged for mercy.

Thus did valiant Aeneas storm through the battlefield dealing out death, until at last young Iulus and his warrior comrades broke forth from the camp and the siege was lifted.

Jupiter was perturbed. He summoned Juno: "You are right. It is the helping hand of Venus that gives the Trojans the advantage. Turnus is destined to die, but in fairness, I grant you the right to put off his fate for a while. Do not think, though, that you can change what is bound to come at last."

Juno wept at the thought of Turnus' doom, but she flew down and conjured up a shadow figure of Aeneas, so convincing that when it goaded Turnus and then fled, the Latin followed in hot pursuit, thinking he had his enemy on the run. The phantom leapt on to a ship anchored offshore, chased on board by Turnus. Juno broke the mooring ropes and drove the ship out to sea, where the shadow of Aeneas fled up and melted into the clouds, leaving Turnus ranting on the deck: "I am shamed… disgraced! My armies will think themselves abandoned!"

With Turnus spirited out of harm's way by Juno, the battle seethed. Trojans and Latins fell in equal numbers. And so at last Mezentius and Aeneas came face to face. Mezentius' first spear bounced off Aeneas' shield. Aeneas felled Mezentius with his own throw, wounding him in the groin. Seizing his sword Aeneas rushed forward. Mezentius' son Lausus now showed great courage – seeing his father's helpless state, he ran up and stood before him, even as the Trojan raised his sword arm to strike. Aeneas cried out to the boy to stand aside, but he would not. So it was that young Lausus died, pierced through by the sword of Aeneas.

Grieving at this death, thinking of his own love for his father, Aeneas lifted Lausus in his arms. He called for the Latins to take his body. Mezentius, wild with sorrow, refused to be held back, despite the anguish of his own wound. He climbed upon his horse and charged at Aeneas, circling him three times and hurling spears which stuck quivering in Aeneas' shield. Aeneas, biding his time, at last threw his own spear, which caught Mezentius' war-horse between the eyes. The animal reared, throwing its rider to the ground, and so Mezentius, like his son, died at the hand of the Trojan leader.

CAMILLA

THE SIEGE OF THE TROJAN CAMP was now lifted as the Latin armies fell back. Aeneas made offerings to the gods and then, in great grief, he ordered the return of the body of Pallas to his mourning father. The funeral bier was escorted by a thousand chosen men, followed by horses and weapons taken from the enemy and by a group of bound captives whose blood would be sprinkled upon the flames.

From the city of the Latins came envoys bearing the olive branch of peace, begging to be allowed to bury their dead. Aeneas received them kindly: "Would that these dead were still alive," he said. "I never sought this slaughter. Fate decreed that we Trojans seek a home in this land – there could have been peace between us, had not your king abandoned the friendship he offered at first and preferred Turnus' frenzy for battle. It is Turnus who should risk his own life. Let him face me in single combat."

The Latins heard this in astonishment, and instantly fell into disagreement among themselves. Drances, a Latin prince who hated Turnus, urged that they should make a treaty with Aeneas on their own account and help the Trojans to build their city: "Let Turnus look after himself. Why should we lay down our lives so that he may have a royal bride?"

The funeral pyres of fallen warriors now blazed upon the plain. Swords and helmets were flung upon the biers, along with chariot wheels, bridles, shields and spears. Three times the mourners ran around the flames, their armour gleaming in the night. And as the flames sank, the glow of a thousand pyres matched the burning stars in the heavens above.

Within the city, the Latins continued to argue. Messengers arrived from King Diomede refusing the reinforcements which Latinus had requested. When the king heard this, he lost heart. "These blows are warnings from the gods. It must indeed be destiny that brings Aeneas to these shores. We are misguided to take up arms against him. Let us propose a treaty and offer lands where the Trojans may raise their city."

Drances was quick to offer his support. "Wisely spoken, O king!" And he swung round to challenge Turnus. "As for you – you are the cause of all our woes! Our finest warriors have spilled their blood for you! And all so that you may get yourself a wife!"

Turnus stood there weary and dishevelled. Juno's strategy to save him from the battlefield had sent him far out to sea, furious and frustrated, before eventually the ship beached many miles away. Hotfoot he had returned, only to find the fighting done and the Trojans once more in control of their camp. Drances' words stirred him into a fine passion: "Scum of the earth! All talk and no action – that's you, Drances!" he shouted. And he forgot his disappointment and his aching limbs as he flew to the attack. "Have you no pride, no spirit! Are we to stand by and see our lands overrun by these Trojans just because a few heads have rolled? We are not without allies. Messapus is here. So is noble Camilla, with her Volscian cavalry. But if Aeneas challenges me, and me alone, then I am ready for the fight and for the glory!"

The Latins were now quite divided, some swayed by Turnus' exhortations, others listening to the king. But even as they argued, a messenger came running up to say that Aeneas had struck camp and was advancing upon the city with all his forces. Turnus seized his moment: "To arms! Defend the approaches! Man the towers!"

Beyond the city gates, Camilla brought forward her squadron. "We are with you, Turnus," she declared. "Let me lead my troops into battle while you mount the defence of the walls."

But Turnus had his own scheme. "I plan an ambush. My scouts tell me that Aeneas plans to advance upon the city himself by way of a ridge along the mountains, while his cavalry pushes forward across the plain. I shall wait for him in the valley below. Go, great princess! Go forth and engage with the Etruscan cavalry!"

Before long, the whole plain was alight with men and horses as the two armies came within a spear's throw of each other. The horses pranced and plunged, uplifted weapons glinted in the sun. And then, with a great shout, the leaders charged, racing towards one another with lances levelled. The battle lines were thrown into confusion, Trojan tangled with Latin. The Latins turned and retreated to the city walls, holding their shields above their backs as protection – only to whirl around and surge back to the attack. To and fro the armies rolled, back and forth, like waves that rush up a shingle beach and then fall back into the sea, sucking the pebbles with them.

In the midst of the tumult rode the Amazon Camilla, exulting in battle. Her quiver was on her shoulder, with the golden bow and arrows of the goddess Diana. Her right arm was bared for action – to catch up her pliant spear, or her mighty double axe. She brought down Eunaeus, then Liris and Pegasus. For every arrow that flew from her bow, a Trojan hero fell. She caught mighty Butes with her spear. Orsilochus pursued her, but she turned his pursuit into flight and split his skull with her axe.

The Etruscan leader Tarchon saw his cohorts in retreat and rode among them, rallying each man by name. "Shame on you – routed by a woman! Use your weapons!" And he drove them back into the fray.

All this while, Arruns was stalking Camilla. He circled her as she fought, watching for his opportunity. And at last the moment came. Hurling his spear, he offered a prayer to Apollo: "Let me be the one to bring down this Amazon... I want no renown for the deed – just to return to my Etruscan home in safety."

His spear struck home. Camilla fell. Her girl companions gathered about her as she lay dying and whispered with her last breath: "All grows dark around me. Take this message to Turnus – he must come to take charge of the battle and keep the Trojans from the walls of the city." So died Camilla, and with her death a great shout rose to the skies.

Arruns had fled from the scene. The god had granted him the first part of his prayer, but not the second. The nymph Opis, sentinel for the goddess Diana, had seen him slay Camilla, beloved of her mistress. She flew down from her vantage point high in the mountains and aimed her golden arrow

at Arruns as he passed by, still exulting at his feat. "Now pay the price for what you have done!" she cried. And so Arruns too lay groaning in the dust.

Now the Latin leaders were in disarray. Camilla's force was the first to flee, then the other leaderless companies made for safety. The thunder of galloping horses drummed across the plain. The Latin women on the ramparts of the city saw clouds of black dust swirl towards them and cried out to the stars in their despair. The first of the fleeing Latin forces burst through the open gates. Others were left outside as those within prepared to defend the city against the advancing Trojans.

News of the rout came to Turnus, waiting still for Aeneas in the valley below the mountains. He hastened at once to take command of the city. No sooner had he done so than Aeneas came over the ridge and down on to the plain. And thus the two made for the walls of the city at the same time and at last set eyes on one another.

It was not the hour for confrontation. Night was falling. Both leaders set up camp before the city to wait for the light of day.

THE DEATH OF TURNUS

TURNUS SAW THAT THE LATINS faced defeat. His own courage surged as he confronted the king. "The time has come. We shall settle this once and for all, Aeneas and I, man to man. Either I slay him, or he rules here and takes Lavinia for his wife."

King Latinus begged him not to waste his life. "It was folly on my part to take up arms against the Trojans. I was swayed by my affection for you. But Lavinia is now plighted to Aeneas – fate decrees it. I am ready for an alliance with the Trojan race."

Turnus would have none of this. "I do not want your concern. Let this final contest decide the war. Allow me a glorious death, if that too is decreed."

He put on his armour – the breastplate with scales of gold and copper, the helmet plumed with red. He took up his spear and sword, blazing with rage and resolution so that he was like some bull primed for a fight, that bellows and paws the ground. His horses were brought to him, the charioteers combing their flowing manes and clapping their hands against the animals' chests to put them on their mettle.

Aeneas too arrayed himself. A field for the duel was measured out on the plain before the city and the men of both armies gathered in two great assemblies, as though lined up for battle, but with their spears planted in the ground and shields propped against them.

Juno looked down in anguish. She spoke to the goddess Juturna. "I can do no more. Go – find a way to snatch your brother from death."

The two leaders advanced. Turnus rode in a chariot drawn by two white horses. The figure of Aeneas gleamed in his miraculous armour, his shield shining out like a star – the shield that predicted the great future of Rome.

Both men made offerings to the gods. Aeneas vowed that if he should be victorious he would not subject the Latins to his own people, but that all should be equal… "And the name of the city we build shall be Lavinium, in honour of the princess." King Latinus in turn swore that the men of Italy would honour this treaty and there should be peace between their peoples.

But while these rituals took place, the watching Latins grew restive. They saw that young Turnus looked less powerful than the great Trojan warrior, and they feared for his defeat. Juturna seized her chance to interfere She moved among the armies disguised as a renowned Latin leader, Camers, sowing rumours: "Look how few are the enemy! We outnumber them by far! Are you not ashamed to sacrifice one man for all of us? Turnus will be famous whatever happens – but if we lose our homeland, we shall be slaves to these invaders!"

At that moment, a golden eagle hunting down by the shore was seen to seize a swan, whereupon a great flock of birds darkened the sky as they mobbed

the eagle, forcing it to drop its prey. The Latins let forth a shout, seeing this as an omen. Wild disorder spread among the ranks of men. Swords were drawn, spears held ready. Skirmishes broke out. Messapus led a charge, eager to break the treaty. The Trojans joined battle. And so, while Aeneas in vain called for a stop to this madness, Trojan and Italian fell once more into frenzied combat.

Aeneas tried in desperation to curb his allies: "We have a treaty! The conflict is mine, and mine alone!" Even as he did so, an assailant took aim. His arrow flew up and came arching down to strike Aeneas in the thigh. The wound was grievous; his distraught companions led him from the field.

Seeing this, Turnus flung himself into the battle with renewed fury and sudden hope. He whipped his horses into the thick of the fight, dealing out blows on all sides, trampling the bodies of the fallen. Wherever he went, the Trojan ranks fell back in disorder at the sight of his whirling figure, the red plumes flying from his helmet.

Aeneas was taken to the Trojan camp with blood streaming from his wound, and raging at his misfortune. His companions gathered round and Iulus stood anxious at his father's side while Iapyx, skilled in medicine, tried in vain to extract the metal barb with instruments. And all the while the battle roared beyond them.

Venus saw what had happened to her son. She flew to Mount Ida in Crete and there plucked leaves of dittany, the scarlet-flowered healing plant. As Iapyx bathed Aeneas' wound, she secretly infused the river water that he used with this herb. And thus the blood was staunched, the pain extinguished and the arrowhead fell from the flesh.

Aeneas called for his arms, impatient to take command once more. He stormed from the camp with his escorting cohorts, and as the Latins saw the dust-clouds of their approach, they in turn fell back in dismay. But Aeneas was hunting for Turnus, and Turnus alone, searching him out amid the tumult.

Juturna was ready with another desperate strategy to preserve her brother's life. She assumed the form of his charioteer Metiscus and seized the reins of his chariot. She whipped up the horses and made the chariot fly like the wind from one part of the battlefield to another, twisting and turning, so that Aeneas would glimpse Turnus, rush in pursuit, and each time lose him in the throng.

Thus the two leaders stayed always at a distance from one another, both of them furiously fighting all who stood in their way, dealing out death and destruction. The opposing armies were locked in combat, neither side giving way, until at last Aeneas turned his eyes to the city, standing there unscathed. He summoned his commanders and ordered an all-out assault upon the walls: "There lies the root of this shameful war! I will wait no longer for Turnus to meet me face to face. Let us enforce our treaty with fire!"

The Trojans formed a wedge and rushed the gates. Ladders swarmed up the ramparts. Firebrands flew. Within the city, all was fear and lamentation.

Far out on the plain, Turnus was rounding up stragglers, angry and frustrated at the wayward and uncontrollable behaviour of his horses. The wind brought to him the shouting from without the city, the wailing of the Latin women within. "What is this!" he cried. "Turn the horses!"

"No, no!" cried Juturna, disguised still as the charioteer. "Your task is out here. You must harry these fleeing Trojans! Others will defend the city."

But Turnus now saw how he had been deceived. "I know you, sister! Would you have me turn tail while our homes are destroyed? And if I die, what is so terrible about that? Dishonour is far worse."

The Latin leaders galloped up on foaming steeds to seek his help. Tongues of flame shot out from the city towers and Turnus leapt from his chariot, crying, "The time has come! I will be shamed no more. I go to meet Aeneas in battle. Put up your swords, comrades!" And with this, he headed for the city. At the sight of him, the armies parted to clear a way.

And so at last the two heroes met on the open ground before the walls of the city. Like two great bulls they circled one another, now exchanging spear-throws, now clashing sword to sword. Turnus rose to his full height for a sword-blow that he thought would end it all, but the sword snapped off as he struck, leaving him with nothing but the hilt. Disarmed, he had to flee, with Aeneas immediately in pursuit. Aeneas flung his spear, thinking in his turn that victory was his. But the spear went wide and stuck fast in the trunk of a wild olive tree.

For one last time the gods moved to protect those they loved. Juturna once more assumed the form of Metiscus the charioteer, and came forward with a new sword for Turnus. Venus flew down to wrench free Aeneas' spear as he struggled vainly to retrieve it.

But Jupiter himself protested, addressing Juno. "Enough! The end is come. Seek no longer to stand in the way of fate. I forbid you to meddle further."

Juno bowed her head. "Yes — it was I who sent Juturna to her brother's rescue. I submit, great Jupiter. So be it. But grant me one prayer. Allow the Latins to keep their ancient name. Troy is come to Italy, but let its name be left where Troy fell. Let this place be called Latium."

Jupiter smiled. "I grant your request. And now, lay aside your anger. You shall see how those descended from this marriage of two bloods will be greatest of all races. And they will offer you great honour."

Still Juturna hovered near her brother. Jupiter summoned one of the monstrous Dirae, who predict death. The demon sped to earth and took the shape of a little bird of ill omen, which flew at Turnus, screeching and battering him with its wings. Turnus was struck with an icy numbness, but Juturna knew the portent for what it was. She beat her breast in grief. "Would that I too might die. But I am condemned to eternal life." And so saying, she covered her head with a blue-green veil and plunged into the depths of her own river.

Aeneas' spear flashed as he challenged Turnus. "Stand and fight!"

"I am not afraid of you!" cried Turnus. "But I fear the gods."

So saying, he bent down and seized a huge boulder, raised it above his head with both arms and ran at full tilt towards the Trojan, hurling the rock at him. But as he did so, he felt himself falter. His knees trembled, the rock fell from his hands and rolled harmlessly aside. Fear swept through him, for he knew that death came stalking his way.

Aeneas aimed his spear. It crashed through the outer rim of Turnus' shield and split his thigh, sending him tumbling to the ground.

The Trojan stood above the fallen Latin, his hand on his sword. Turnus groaned: "I have brought this upon myself. Relish your good fortune. Lavinia is yours. But take pity on my grieving father, I beg you. Return me to him and to my people – or return my dead body, if that is what you wish."

Aeneas hesitated, moved by his words and considering mercy. And then his eye was caught by something that glittered on Turnus' shoulder: the studs upon Pallas' belt – the belt snatched from his body by Turnus after he slew him.

The Trojan's fury surged once more. "Die! It is Pallas who exacts revenge!" He sank his blade into the man at his feet. The limbs of Turnus froze in death, and his angry soul fled groaning to the Underworld.

EPILOGUE

S O IT WAS THAT FROM the ashes of Troy Aeneas led his people to a new homeland. Many brave men had shed their blood in the struggle, but now there was peace between Trojan and Latin.

After the death of his father, Iulus founded a city, Alba Longa. In time to come, there rose in that place glorious Rome herself, splendid in her monuments and in the wisdom of her great rulers – an empire that was to reach the length and breadth of the ancient world.

LIGURIA

LIBURNIA

ETRURIA

UMBRIA

River Tiber

Adriatic Sea

Pallanteum (Rome) • Alba Longa
LATIUM

VOLSCIANS

Cumae•

APULIA

N

Tyrrhenian
Sea

Cape Palinurus

AEOLIA

Ionian
Sea

SILA

Drepanum• •Eryr

Mt
Etna•

SICILIA

•Carthage

LIBYA

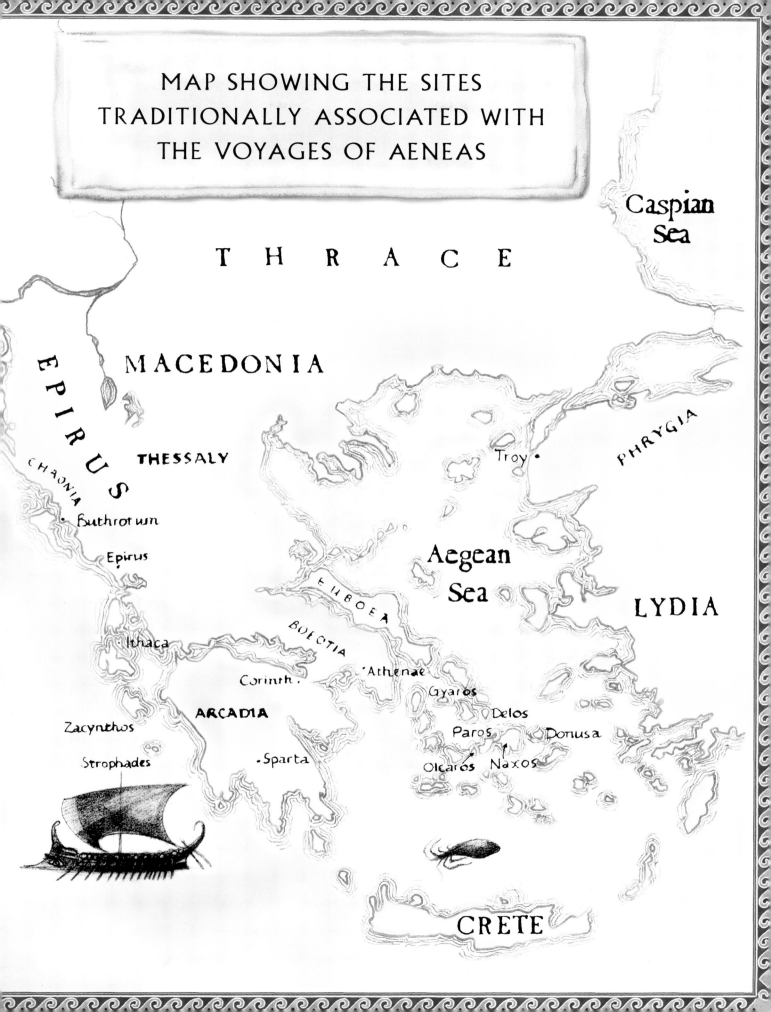

MAP SHOWING THE SITES TRADITIONALLY ASSOCIATED WITH THE VOYAGES OF AENEAS

Caspian Sea

T H R A C E

MACEDONIA

EPIRUS

THESSALY

CHAONIA

Buthrotum

Epirus

PHRYGIA

Troy

Aegean Sea

LYDIA

EUBOEA

BOEOTIA

Ithaca

Corinth

Athenae

Gyaros

Delos

ARCADIA

Paros

Donusa

Zacynthos

Olearos

Naxos

Strophades

Sparta

CRETE

HOW TO PRONOUNCE THE GREEK AND LATIN NAMES

The letter *e* is pronounced long, as in "me", but when marked *ĕ* it is pronounced short, as in "wet".

The letters *i* and *y* are pronounced *ea* as in "bead", or *i* as in "bin".

The letters *eu* together are pronounced like the word "you".

The letters *au* together are pronounced *ow* as in "how".

The letters *ae*, *oe*, *ei* together are pronounced like the *e* in "me".

The letters *ch* are pronounced like *c*, as in "chord".

The letter *g* is pronounced like *j*, as in "giant".

The letters *rh* are pronounced like *r*, as in "rat".

The accent is on the syllable marked ´.

These are some of the more difficult pronunciations:

Achátes	Délos
Achílles	Dído
Aenéas	Eurýalus
Anchíses	Evánder
Andrómache	Iúlus
Bĕro-e	Iutúrna
Cácus	La-ocó-on
Charýbdis	Latínus
Círce	Latium
Cre-úsa	Laúsus
Cúmae	Minérva
Dáres	Mycénae

Nísus

Príam

Pýrrhus

Scýlla (silla)

Sínon

Styx

Sychaéus

Tĕnĕdos

Ulýsses

Traditional English pronunciation is generally used for the following names: Anchises, Dido, Mycenae, Priam — the letters *i* and *y* are pronounced as in "eye".
Circe, Mycenae — the letter *c* is pronounced "s".

Virgil's *The Aeneid*, translated by C. Day Lewis (Oxford University Press, 1952), W.F. Jackson Knight (Penguin, 1956), Robert Fitzgerald (Penguin, 1985) and David West (Penguin, 1991).

The Greek Myths, by Robert Graves (Penguin, 1955).

An Introduction to Virgil's Aeneid, by W.A. Camps (Oxford University Press, 1969).

Virgil: His Poetry Through the Ages, by R.D. Williams and T.S. Pattie (The British Library, 1982).